An impossible mission

I lay on my bed for a minute and shut my eyes. The situation wasn't hopeless, was it? Sometimes celebrities did charity visits. Maybe the Make-A-Wish Foundation could help. That was the sort of thing they did. Would four days be long enough to process a request? It seemed like such a short time, but if Steve Raleigh knew, if someone explained the situation to him, surely he would want to help out, wouldn't he?

Four days.

I Googled "Set location for Teen Robin Hood" and immediately came up with pictures of Ballard Productions in Burbank, California.

I stared at those for a long time, letting ideas congeal into possibilities. Could I call them and ask to speak to Steve? No, that wouldn't work. The only way I'd ever be able to convince him to help me on such short notice was if I asked him in person.

Finally I came up with a plan. It was desperate, stupid, and obviously impossible for the average teenage girl. But in the end, that was the thing that tipped the scales. If anyone could figure out a way to breach that impenetrable wall, I could. At least, I hoped I could. Actually, I didn't want to think about my chances. I just had to go and do it.

OTHER BOOKS YOU MAY ENJOY

JANETTE RALLISON

speak
An Imprint of Penguin Group (USA) Inc.

SPEAK
Published by the Penguin Group
Penguin Group (USA) Inc., 345 Hudson Street, New York, New York 10014, U.S.A.
Penguin Group (Canada), 90 Eglinton Avenue East, Suite 700, Toronto, Ontario, Canada M4P 2Y3
(a division of Pearson Penguin Canada Inc.)
Penguin Books Ltd, 80 Strand, London WC2R 0RL, England
Penguin Ireland, 25 St Stephen's Green, Dublin 2, Ireland (a division of Penguin Books Ltd)
Penguin Group (Australia), 250 Camberwell Road, Camberwell, Victoria 3124, Australia
(a division of Pearson Australia Group Pty Ltd)
Penguin Books India Pvt Ltd, 11 Community Centre, Panchsheel Park, New Delhi - 110 017, India
Penguin Group (NZ), 67 Apollo Drive, Rosedale, North Shore 0632, New Zealand
(a division of Pearson New Zealand Ltd)
Penguin Books (South Africa) (Pty) Ltd, 24 Sturdee Avenue, Rosebank, Johannesburg 2196, South Africa

Registered Offices: Penguin Books Ltd, 80 Strand, London WC2R 0RL, England

First published in the United States of America by G. P. Putnam's Sons,
a division of Penguin Young Readers Group, 2009

Published by Speak, an imprint of Penguin Group (USA) Inc., 2010

1 3 5 7 9 10 8 6 4 2

THE LIBRARY OF CONGRESS HAS CATALOGED THE PUTNAM EDITION AS FOLLOWS:
Rallison, Janette, date.
Just one wish / Janette Rallison. p. cm.
Summary: Seventeen-year-old Annika tries to cheer up her little brother Jeremy
before his surgery to remove a cancerous tumor by bringing home
his favorite television actor, Steve Raleigh, the star of "Teen Robin Hood."
ISBN: 978-0-399-24618-0 (hc)
[1. Brothers and sisters—Fiction. 2. Cancer—Fiction. 3. Actors and actresses—Fiction.]
I. Title.
PZ7.R13455Ju 2009 [Fic]—dc22 2008009297

Speak ISBN 978-0-14-241599-3

Printed in the United States of America

To my husband, Guy,
who got the children off to school every day
so I could stay up late writing. That is true love.

Also to my editor, Tim, who pushes me to reach further
and dig deeper where my writing is concerned. Of course,
he has also been known to expect me to walk into the street
in front of oncoming traffic . . . so, you know,
his judgment can't always be trusted. . . .

Special thanks to Eric Murdock for answering my mechanic
questions and to Bill Gardner, who knows way too much
about driving cars over medians and other places that they
don't belong—and who probably knows too much about me as well.

Also thanks to Linda Ballard and Richard Hatch for
answering my questions about what happens on a studio set.
Hollywood insiders are harder to catch than leprechauns.

Thanks to Steve Crawley for being the best flyer/poster/bookmark
man in the world. I owe you way more than brownies.

And lastly to Spencer Cowgill and BJ Abney,
children cancer took too soon.

Chapter 1

$\mathcal{I}$ would have expected to see this sort of line if, say, Elvis had returned from the dead to give a concert. Or if some eccentric yet ultra-cool billionaire was blessing the lives of deserving teens by handing out free sports cars. But I hadn't expected to see this many people lined up in the dark waiting for the Day-After-Thanksgiving sale at Toys "R" Us. Really, whatever happened to good old-fashioned procrastination? Apparently every resident of Henderson, Nevada, had come out, and it was still only 4:50 A.M. The store didn't even open for another ten minutes.

Madison zipped her jacket up higher as we climbed out of my minivan. "This is a prime example of commercialism run amok."

I didn't answer, because I was too busy rushing across the parking lot to the end of the line. Besides, Madison really shouldn't talk—every year she gets so many gifts you have to listen to her complain until New Year's about how she has to reorganize her room to fit them all in.

Madison is not only my best friend, but probably the only friend I could convince to get up this early to track down a Talking Teen Robin Hood action figure for my six-year-old brother. I myself wouldn't have woken up at four-thirty if it weren't so important.

Madison folded her arms around herself for warmth. We'd only worn light jackets because we hadn't expected to wait outside very long, but even the Nevada desert is cold at ten to five in the morning. Madison's usually tidy shoulder-length hair—she calls it strawberry blond, but it is way more strawberry than blond—looked as though she hadn't even combed it. I'd thrown on sweats and shoved my hair into a ponytail. Now I wished I'd thought to bring a hat.

Madison peered at the line in front of us. "You know, Annika, if you can't find a Teen Robin Hood, I'm sure Jeremy would be fine with a different gift. Maybe you could get him a real bow and arrow set like yours."

I thought about my compound bow, but I couldn't imagine Jeremy with something like that. It was nearly as big as he was, and he might not have the strength to pull it back all the way. The thought made my throat feel tight.

I shook my head. "It has to be Teen Robin Hood."

Jeremy had said he wanted the Teen Robin Hood action figure, and kept saying it every time he watched the TV show, so that was the toy I had to get him.

The husband and wife in front of us were busy planning their buying strategy. "I'll call you as soon as I have the PlayStation in my hands. You grab one of those bikes that's on sale. Throw yourself over it if you have to."

I pulled my sleeves over my hands to keep out the chill. Why did Jeremy have to love Robin Hood? Why couldn't he still want to be Hercules? I bet you no one was throwing themselves over the Hercules toys.

At five o'clock the doors opened, but it took us another twenty minutes to get in. By that time the aisles buzzed with people grabbing toys from shelves, and lines had already formed at the registers.

I told Madison, "Why don't you go stand in line while I look for action figures. It will take less time that way."

I didn't wait for her answer, just weaved my way down an aisle. I wanted to hurry past people but continually found myself trapped behind carts with mammoth toys that blocked the way.

I cut across the Barbie doll aisle and momentarily considered picking up a girlfriend for Teen Robin Hood, one who was a little more suitable for him than Maid Marion. I'm sorry, but the actress who plays her is a total flake. All she does is flutter, cry, and wait for rescue. She never would have made it two days in the real Middle Ages, which is why I started rooting for Robin Hood to dump her after the third episode. I bet even Barbie could have taken her on in a serious smack down.

Finally I found the action figure row. I walked up and down, scanning the shelves for the green boxes of the Nottingham characters. The four-inch set Jeremy already owned sat prominently on the shelf, but I didn't see the new, larger twelve-inch version, which was supposed to be available starting today.

Where were they?

The store couldn't be sold out on the first day at five-twenty-five in the morning, could they? Shouldn't they have a large shipment sitting around? I went to the next aisle. Nothing. And then I saw the endcap and the shelves of Nottingham green boxes.

A man with a dozen boxes in his shopping cart stood sifting through them. He wore a fake leather jacket that stretched over his stomach and an opal ring so large you could have used it as a serving tray.

I jogged over to the display, my eyes scanning the boxes for a Robin Hood. Maid Marion, Maid Marion, Little John, the Sheriff. . . .

"Are there any Robin Hoods left?" I asked.

He didn't glance at me, just kept picking up boxes and checking them.

"I think I got them all."

"What? I need one for my little brother."

Now he glanced at me, his gaze sizing me up. "Then you're in luck. I'll sell you one for a hundred and fifty dollars."

"A hundred and fifty? They cost thirty-nine."

"Not once they go in my shopping cart. Then they're a hundred and fifty." He sent an oily smile in my direction. "That's the free market, kid."

I could see the boxes in his cart. They were so close.

I turned to the man, finally giving him my full attention. My mother claims I have a sixth sense about people. I know right after meeting someone what they're like, how perceptive they are, and what makes them tick.

When I was little, I used to wish I had some sort of superpower. I wanted to fly like Superman or climb up buildings like Spider-Man. But when you come right down to it, there aren't a lot of practical applications for superpowers. Being able to read people, however, comes in handy. It helps me deal with teachers and navigate through high school. I pretty much know what I can get away with.

Looking at this man now, I flipped through the possibilities in my mind. He wasn't the type—even if I had been wearing makeup—that I could swish my long blond hair around and he'd relent on his price because a pretty girl asked him. Money motivated him, and nothing but. I didn't detect even an ounce of sympathy circulating through his heart, but still I tried. I would tell him about Jeremy and hope for once I was wrong.

With my hands out pleading, I said, "Look, my brother is sick; he has cancer, and he really wants a Teen Robin Hood. Can't you let me have just one?"

"For a hundred and fifty dollars, I can."

I took out my wallet, and pulled out four twenties. "This is all I have, and I'm going to need forty dollars to buy it at the register."

He snorted and went back to the boxes. "Then maybe your parents can find one on eBay. Of course they might be more than a hundred and fifty there. Robin Hood is the hot toy this season."

I shoved my wallet back into my coat pocket and turned to the shelf. If he was still looking through the boxes, then so would I. There might be one left.

There had to be one left.

I flipped through King John, Friar Tuck, Maid Marion—even her plastic figurine looked like it was about to faint momentarily—the Sheriff, another Friar Tuck, and Robin Hood. Robin Hood! I gasped and grabbed the box.

Unfortunately the man reached for it at the same time and yanked it out of my hands.

"Hey!" I yelled. "That was mine."

"Sorry, kid. I was here first. Besides," he smiled as he grasped the box, "possession is nine tenths of the law."

I peered around the store to see if any employees stood nearby—anyone who had seen him tear the box from my hands and who could help me. But all I saw were other shoppers who were too busy to notice me. This is one more reason why real life is nothing like the Robin Hood series.

The man went back to sifting through the rest of the boxes, chuckling, but he kept one hand on his cart, protecting it.

Madison is a big believer in karma. She doesn't think she ever needs to take revenge because sooner or later bad deeds catch up with people. I have my doubts about the concept. If it were true, wouldn't guys like this get struck down by meteorites?

Anyway, I figured it was time to hurry karma along. I took a step toward him. "Have you ever played football?"

He glanced at me suspiciously. "Sure."

I let my gaze fall on his bulging stomach. "But I bet you haven't played for a while."

"What does that matter?"

"Because I can outrun and outdodge you, especially with that shopping cart."

He caught my meaning as soon as I spoke. I faked to my right. He moved to block me. I spun left, grabbed a Robin Hood from his cart, and dashed away.

My older sister, Leah—who has never touched a football because it might break her fingernails—says I've wasted most of my adolescence playing sports, but this is obviously not true. Running through the store toward the checkout line was just like running for a touchdown, except the other shoppers didn't try to tackle me. Only the man in the fake leather jacket barreled toward me, but he wouldn't let go of his shopping cart, so he kept getting caught up behind other carts.

I lost him long before I found Madison. She stood in the checkout line, now within sight of the registers.

"Here, buy this." I shoved the box and my wallet into her arms. "And don't let some overweight, half-psychotic man in a black jacket take it away from you. Start screaming if he tries."

Her eyes widened in panic, and she clutched the box to her chest. "Annika, what did you do?"

"Nothing." I checked over my shoulder for any signs of him. "Well, nothing Robin Hood wouldn't have done. I'll wait outside."

Then I ran to the exit before she could ask more questions.

I waited in my minivan with the doors locked. Not that I expected the man to come outside looking for me. I knew he wouldn't leave the store without his stash of Robin Hoods, and there was no way he'd get through the checkout line before Madison.

Still, it always pays to be cautious.

I sat huddled in the driver's seat, looking at the dark sky and wishing that clouds hadn't covered up the stars. Clouds always made it seem more like winter and less like Nevada.

Madison came out twenty minutes later. I unlocked the door, and she slid into the front seat, then relocked her door. She handed me the shopping bag and sent me a long gaze. "So do you want to tell me why an angry man pushing Robin Hood boxes around the store kept yelling, 'Come out and show yourself, you punk! You can't hide forever!'"

"Not really." I looked inside the bag, just long enough to make sure it held Robin Hood, then I started the van.

"You risked my life for a stupid toy, didn't you?"

"No. He didn't know I gave you the toy. Besides, he wouldn't have hurt you with all of those witnesses around."

Madison fastened her seat belt. "The veins were popping out of his neck. A couple of employees went over to talk to him, and he yelled about thieves in the store, then threatened to sue them for their lack of security."

I pulled out of the parking lot, checking to make sure no headlights suddenly flicked on and followed me. Only a few cars moved through the street, and I pressed down on the gas, urging the van to go faster so I could zip around them. "Technically I didn't steal from him.

It's like he told me when he ripped the box out of my hands first. Possession is nine tenths of the law."

Madison folded her arms, her disapproval clearly etched on her face. "You don't need to turn shopping into some sort of extreme sport, Annika. It's not supposed to be a duel to the death."

"Jeremy wants the Talking Teen Robin."

"He also wants to live on Sesame Street, you can't just—" Her expression softened. In the space of one breath, her voice changed from berating to reassuring. "Jeremy is going to be okay. Lots of people with cancer recover completely. He probably has better odds than, say, anyone who rides in a car with you."

I took my foot off the gas and let the van slow down but didn't answer her. People kept telling me that Jeremy would be okay. He had top-notch doctors. Cancer treatments improved all the time. He was young and resilient. My parents were unfailingly optimistic in front of me—which was perhaps why I had my doubts. I knew they were faking it. Jeremy's situation was more serious than they let on.

They were especially worried about his upcoming surgery next Friday to remove the tumor from his brain. Mom could hardly speak about it without tensing up. This is the downside of being able to read people. Sometimes it's better not to know when your parents are lying to you.

Madison glanced at me, her voice a mixture of frustration and sympathy. "Look, Annika, no matter what you get Jeremy for Christmas, he'll still know you love him."

I shifted in my seat, looking determinedly out at the traffic. I didn't want to talk about Jeremy or his cancer anymore. I didn't want to think about the fear that daily found its way into his eyes, or the way he automatically panicked when you mentioned doctors. A month and a half of chemo treatments had made him hate hospitals. Last night he told my mom he didn't want to go to bed, because if he did, it would mean surgery was one day closer.

Out of the blue, he said things like, "Do people get to fly after they die, or only the angels?" Other times he swayed back and forth with worry and told us he didn't want to get buried in the ground. He knew it would be cold and dark there. I don't even know where he learned about cemeteries. None of us talked about that sort of thing. But now he refused to turn off the light when he slept.

"Besides," Madison went on, "he probably won't care about that toy two days after he opens it. If you want to do something nice, then spend a few hours playing with him. That would mean more to him than anything you could buy at a store."

She made me sound like one of those neglectful parents who ignores their children and then tries to buy their affection.

"Just drop it," I said. "You don't understand about this."

"What's not to understand? It's a textbook case of trying to shop away your feelings. People do it all the time, and I'm just saying—"

Right. I refused to believe someone could flip through a book and come to the chapter on how I felt. "Stop it," I said. "Until your little brother has cancer, don't tell me how I feel."

Neither of us spoke for a few seconds. Madison looked out the window with her lips drawn into a tight line. "Sorry," she said in a clipped tone. "I was trying to help."

I knew I had overreacted. It seemed like I'd done nothing but overreact since we'd gotten the news in mid-October. I snapped at people who reassured me. I argued with people who offered me comfort.

I knew I should apologize to Madison, but I couldn't do it. We drove through the streets of Henderson watching the darkness fade away, pierced by the rising sun. We still didn't speak. Madison turned on the radio, but the music didn't chase away the silence between us. I pulled up in front of her house.

"Thanks for coming with me," I said.

She reached for the door handle. "No problem. It was

fun. Especially the part where I had to shield your action figure with my body so Mr. Gargoyle wouldn't see it as he stormed around the store."

I let out a sigh. "Just because the guy was unbalanced doesn't mean he would have killed you."

"Of course not." She flung the door open. "Besides, I think it's a good thing to face death every once in a while. It makes you appreciate life all the more." She paused halfway out of the van and looked back at me, her face ashen. "I'm sorry, Annika. I didn't mean that."

I hadn't even connected the two subjects in my mind, and my heart squeezed painfully in my chest. "Stop apologizing. Jeremy's not going to die."

"I know. That's what I keep telling you."

"I'll talk to you later," I said. I just wanted to leave.

"Right. We'll get together and do something."

"Right."

She shut the door. I pulled away from her house too fast, which was usual, and gripped the steering wheel white-knuckled, which wasn't. As I drove home, I took deep breaths and glanced at the shopping bag on the seat next to me. This would work. I'd read dozens of stories about how positive thinking had saved people's lives. I'd read studies saying the same thing. *Cancer Research* magazine said that reducing stress could slow the spread of some cancers.

And even researchers who doubted the link between

positive thinking and healing couldn't deny the placebo effect. When doctors give participants of drug tests placebos, there are always a certain percentage of people who get better simply because they think they're taking medicine. Their belief heals them.

If a sugar pill can make an adult get better, then Jeremy could get better if he really believed it. All I had to do was to convince him he'd come through surgery with flying colors, and he would.

If the surgery was successful next Friday—if they were able to take out the entire tumor—then everything would be fine. But if they couldn't remove it all, or something went wrong—I didn't even want to think about the fact that sometimes people died on the operating table. I had to think positively too.

Chapter **2**

$\mathcal{I}$ pulled up to our house, a one-story beige stucco in a row of nearly identical homes. The Nevada heat doesn't allow for much diversity in building materials, and our home owners association doesn't allow for much diversity in anything else. I swear, my parents put out the mat that reads, THE TRUMANS WELCOME YOU just to make sure we were walking into the right place. But over the last month, I can't shake the feeling our house has changed. Sometimes I look at it and it feels like I'm looking at a picture, at a mirage, something that might disappear when you blink. One day I'll drive home and there will only be a vacant lot there.

The garage was empty. My parents must have gone out to brave the crowds too. I made a beeline for my bedroom, shoved my shopping bag in the closet, and went back to bed.

Three hours later, I woke up to the sound of things

clanking in the kitchen and Jeremy yelling at the TV. He seems to think his video games work better if he shouts while playing them.

I pulled myself out of bed, then took the Teen Robin Hood out of the bag to reassure myself I'd really gotten it. I hadn't examined the toy closely before, but the action figure did bear a striking resemblance to Steve Raleigh, the actor who played Robin Hood. It had the same blond hair, square jaw, and perfectly handsome features. His warm brown eyes gazed back at me with an expression of confidence, and I could almost imagine him strutting around Sherwood Forest ordering Merry Men around.

I stared at it a while longer. Probably longer than is normal for a seventeen-year-old girl to stare at a plastic doll. Sometimes when I watch *Teen Robin Hood*—and, okay, I admit I've never missed an episode—I feel a connection with Steve Raleigh. I feel like he's someone I already know, someone who fits with me.

I can't explain it better than that; to tell you the truth, I'm not sure I'm actually reading him right anyway. It's more likely my connection is with Robin Hood. I admire a person who devotes his life to justice, who can live off the land, and who still looks hot after sleeping in the forest. That's real talent.

Steve Raleigh, on the other hand, is probably one of

those pampered celebrities who never sets foot in the grocery store, let alone the wilderness.

I slid the box under my bed for later. I would wait until Jeremy and I were alone, until everything was perfect and my plan couldn't go wrong. Then I would give it to him.

When I went into the kitchen, Dad and Mom were cleaning up dishes from a pancake breakfast, Jeremy's favorite. Although now Mom bought the pancake mix and syrup from an organic health-food store. She won't serve anything that's not 100 percent natural anymore.

"Hey, Sleeping Beauty," Dad called to me. "We saved you a couple, but you'll need to heat them up."

Mom crossed the kitchen and gave me a hug. She insists on hugging us every day. She read it's good for your immune system. "Did you get any good bargains?"

I picked up a pancake and took a bite. "Actually, I made out like a bandit. How about you guys?"

"I got some good deals." Mom lowered her voice and looked toward the family room where Jeremy sat planted in front of the TV. "I couldn't find a Teen Robin Hood anywhere. We told Jeremy the stores were all sold out and so now he wants to go to the mall to ask Santa for one." Her eyes crinkled with worry.

"Don't worry," I said, trying to downplay my smile. "Something might turn up."

"Oh?" Mom waited for me to explain, but when I didn't, she didn't question me further. After I'd eaten breakfast, I played *Super Mario Kart* with Jeremy for a couple hours. I tried to get Leah to play so I could take a break, but she was too busy simultaneously tying up our phone line and text-messaging people on her cell phone.

Leah goes to the College of Southern Nevada. Which basically means she lives with us but is disdainful about being forced into spending time with us. Usually when she's not at class she's out somewhere working on her social life.

People say I look like Leah, and I take it as a compliment. The difference is, beauty and flirting have always come naturally to Leah. Everything I know on both subjects, I've copied from her. Sometimes when I'm with guys, I'm not sure if I'm being myself or just channeling my sister. I'd rather play basketball with guys than bat my eyelashes at them.

When Jeremy got tired of crashing cars off the raceway, I challenged him to an archery match. We set up the target near the wall at our property's edge, then Jeremy stood ten feet away and I stood twenty. I didn't use my compound for this game. We both used Jeremy's junior archery set to make it fair. Every time we hit the mark, we took a step backward. Whoever missed first lost.

I should mention I'm president of the archery club. As my parents put it, I excel at the sport. I'm the only one in our family who can stand out on the sidewalk in front of the house, with the front and back doors open, and hit a target in the backyard.

Today as I played with Jeremy, I only took a few steps and purposely missed.

"I can't believe it," I told him. "I think the target jumped out of the way or something. If you make your next shot, you'll beat me."

He glanced at me, then pulled his arrow back on the string. I could tell he wasn't aiming. His arrow fell short of the target by over a foot.

"Buddy, did you even try?" I asked.

He shrugged. "It's okay, Annika. I know you like to win."

His words made me catch my breath. "No, I . . ." I couldn't say anything else for a moment. "I don't always have to win."

But that's the problem. You can't erase a competitive nature with one day. All I could do was change the subject. As I pulled arrows off the target, I said, "Hey, isn't it about time to watch what's happening in Sherwood Forest?"

He tilted his head as though I should know better. "Not until after dinner."

I did know better. I just wanted to change the subject

to Robin Hood. "Good. We don't want to miss it. Robin Hood is really cool, huh?"

Jeremy walked over to the target and picked up the arrows from the ground. "I'm gonna get a Talking Teen Robin Hood for Christmas. His bow works for real."

I walked toward the house and motioned for him to follow me. "Let's go into my room. I want to tell you a secret."

He trotted after me into the house, his bow still in hand. When we got to my room, I sat cross-legged on my bed. He climbed up next to me, fingering the string on his bow and looking serious. "What's your secret?"

I leaned toward him, my voice low. "Well, I've never told anyone this before, but years ago I found a magic lamp, the kind genies live in. I rubbed the lamp, released the genie, and got three wishes. But I didn't use them all. I still have two left."

Jeremy tilted his chin down, and his lips momentarily scrunched together. "I'm in first grade, Annika. I know there's no such thing as genies."

This from the boy who wanted to ask Santa for his action figure and who, when questioned, said he was going to become a Merry Man when he grew up.

"It's true," I insisted. "I have two wishes left, and I want to give them to you."

His eyes narrowed skeptically. "What was your first wish?"

"Um. . . ." You'd think I would have thought of an answer to this question, but I hadn't. I mean what six-year-old when given two wishes asks you what you wished for?

"I'll tell you some other time. Right now I want to explain the rules about wishing because you can't wish for more wishes or for impossible stuff like superpowers. And don't even think about wishing to fly, because my genie is one of those difficult genies, and he might turn you into a bird or something."

Jeremy looked thoughtful, and I added, "Mom would be very upset if you turned into a bird, and then I'd have to use the last wish turning you back human again. It would be a total waste of wishes. I want you to use the last wish to make sure the surgery will go fine. That way you won't have to worry about it anymore."

"Why don't I wish that I don't have to have the surgery in the first place?" he asked, and his eyes lit up at this prospect.

It hurt to have to disappoint him. "Mom and Dad would make you have the surgery anyway. They don't believe in genies, so it wouldn't matter what we told them about it. It's better just to wish it will go fine."

Jeremy nodded, accepting this explanation, then looked back at me with skeptical eyes. "Annika, are you tricking me?"

"No. Now shut your eyes and say, 'This is my official

second wish,' and wish for something you really want. You'll see I'm telling the truth." I leaned toward him, my eyes never leaving his. "What toy would you most like to have right now?"

He shut his eyes. "Do I have to call the genie first?"

"He'll come when you say, 'This is my official second wish.' That's why you have to shut your eyes. He's shy around anyone who didn't rub his lamp. You're not supposed to see him."

Jeremy opened one eye a sliver.

"Shut your eyes all the way," I told him.

"I can't help myself. I've never seen a genie before."

I gave him a stern look. "It won't work if you don't shut your eyes. The genie will stomp off and you'll lose your wishes."

Jeremy shut his eyes but tilted his head. "He'll stomp off? Do genies have feet?"

"Yes. Well, sort of, anyway." I put my hand under the bed, ready to grab the Robin Hood box. "Now what's your official wish? Think of something you really, really want."

He fidgeted, thinking, then clamped his hands together in decision. "This is my official second wish. I wish the real Teen Robin Hood—the one on TV—would come and teach me how to shoot arrows."

I didn't move. My hand froze over the box, still

wanting to grab it, even though there wasn't a reason to. I felt like the breath had been punched from my lungs.

Jeremy opened his eyes and looked around the room. "Shouldn't something have happened?"

Yes, I should have considered the possibility he'd ask for something besides the action figure. But how could I have known? It's all he'd talked about for the last two weeks.

"Where's Teen Robin Hood?" Jeremy asked. I could see the disappointment seep into his large brown eyes. "You were just tricking me, weren't you?"

"No," I said. "I forgot to tell you that you have to put a time frame on these wishes. You didn't tell the genie when you wanted Teen Robin Hood to come. He might show up tomorrow, a year from now, or when you're sixty-five."

Jeremy's mouth dropped open in frustration, then snapped shut again. "I'll use the third wish to say now."

"No," I yelped. "The third wish has to be for your surgery. I won't give you the third wish until right before then."

Jeremy fingered the string on his bow, and I could tell he was deciding whether to believe me or not. "Genies ought to know you want your wish right away. Haven't they been doing this for a long time?"

"Yes, but I told you this one was difficult. Hopefully it will happen soon . . . ," I said.

The corners of his mouth tugged down. "The genie will probably mess up the surgery wish too."

What had I done? "No, he won't," I said quickly. "We'll make sure he gets it right."

Jeremy lifted his gaze to mine, and I could tell he wanted to believe me but wasn't sure. He picked up the bow lying beside him on my comforter. "Maybe I should practice some more. Maybe when Robin Hood sees how good I am he'll make me a Merry Man."

"Maybe," I said.

He slid from my bed and walked to the door.

"Don't tell Mom and Dad about this," I told him. "You know how they feel about strangers in the house. They'd be mad if they knew a genie was hanging around."

Jeremy nodded and left the room.

I lay on my bed for a minute and shut my eyes. The situation wasn't hopeless, was it? Sometimes celebrities did charity visits. Maybe the Make-A-Wish Foundation could help. That was the sort of thing they did. Of course, no one would be in their office until Monday, so I couldn't even ask them until then, and he had to go in for surgery on Friday morning. Would four days be long enough to process a request? It seemed like such a short time, but if Steve Raleigh knew, if someone explained the situation to him, surely he would want to help out, wouldn't he?

Four days.

I lay on my bed thinking about movie stars. Exactly how busy were they while shooting TV shows? Did they ever do spontaneous things for fans? Were they overwhelmed by requests like these?

The more I thought about it all, the more impossible it seemed. But I had to at least try.

I went to the den and sat in front of the family computer. Maybe I could find some information about Steve Raleigh and contact him myself. When I Googled his name, I got 300,000 links. I clicked on a couple randomly, but they were just chat boards where girls went on and on about how hot Steve was. I clicked on a few with Robin Hood in the title, but they were nothing but pictures of the cast and Hollywood gossip. Mostly pages of discussion dedicated to the question: was Steve Raleigh seeing the actress who played Maid Marion, Esme Kingsley, to get back at his rocker ex-girlfriend, Karli Roller?

Honestly, who cared? Well, besides Esme, Steve, and possibly Karli.

I located the Steve Raleigh fan club. It had a picture of him as Robin Hood, arm muscles rippling as he pulled back an arrow on his longbow. I dragged my gaze away from the picture of Steve and looked for contact information. I didn't see an e-mail address anywhere, but you could write to him care of some guy named Spanky Tyler in Burbank, California. I tried to find a phone number for Spanky by calling directory assistance, but they didn't have a listing.

So, I wrote Spanky a letter telling him about Jeremy. I enclosed a picture, my phone number, and a long plea begging for him to call me. I would overnight it and hope it would be opened first thing Monday morning. I knew it was a long shot—but the thing about long shots is sometimes when you're lucky they still hit the bull's-eye.

The rest of the weekend trickled by. It became more and more painful to watch Jeremy's expectant expression, to have him whisper to me, "Have you heard from the genie yet? Did he say when Robin Hood is coming?"

I called Make-A-Wish as soon as their office opened on Monday, ditching class in the process. I stood inside the girls' bathroom while I explained my brother's wish to the woman on the end of the line. She was sympathetic, but she told me the foundation had to talk to Jeremy's doctor, parents, and to Jeremy himself before they could even begin to process his wish.

I knew it couldn't possibly all happen before Friday, but I still had to ask anyway. "If that was done right away, how long would it take?"

"Wish times vary," she said. "Meeting celebrities—well, that always takes longer. We have to wait for agents to get back to us and then it really depends on the celebrity's schedule. Sometimes they're booked for months."

In other words, not a chance that this could happen before Friday.

When I got home, I carried my cell phone around for hours, hoping Spanky had opened my letter and would give me a call. How much mail did Spanky get in an average day?

No one called, though.

I didn't sleep much that night, although this wasn't unusual. Since Jeremy's diagnosis, my mind couldn't turn off for long enough to sleep. A constant stream of what-ifs kept me awake.

No one called on Tuesday either.

As I sat in class Wednesday morning, I felt like red tape was crawling up my legs, winding around my body, squeezing my chest so tightly that I couldn't breathe. I knew I had to do something. I couldn't just sit there and accept defeat.

After third period, I forged a note telling the office I had a doctor's appointment and went home. Then I sat in our empty house staring at the computer like it was an enemy prisoner. Somewhere amongst its billions of links, it had information that could help me. I had to go about it another way, think of a different way to come at the problem.

I Googled "Set location for Teen Robin Hood" and immediately came up with pictures of Ballard Productions in Burbank, California.

I stared at those for a long time, letting ideas congeal into possibilities. Could I call them and ask to speak to Steve? No, that wouldn't work. There was a huge, impenetrable wall put up around celebrities. Besides, it would be too easy to brush off a stranger calling on the phone. The only way I'd ever be able to convince him to help me on such short notice was if I asked him in person.

Finally I came up with a plan. It was desperate, stupid, and obviously impossible for the average teenage girl. But in the end, that was the thing that tipped the scales. If anyone could figure out a way to breach that impenetrable wall, I could. At least, I hoped I could. Actually, I didn't want to think about my chances. I just had to go and do it.

I printed out directions from Henderson, Nevada, to Burbank, California—a four-hour trip—and texted Madison while I packed things into my duffel bag. "I need your help for a cover. I'm going to tell my parents I'm sleeping over at your house tonight."

Instead of texting back, she called me. I could hear

the background voices and general clanging of the cafeteria. "So, Annika, what are you really doing tonight?"

"Oh, it's this thing I have to do. It's private."

"I'm your best friend. You can tell me." Her voice sounded suspicious. "You're not going to do anything stupid, are you? You're not meeting a guy or something."

I put my toothbrush and toothpaste into the duffel bag. "No, nothing like that. You don't have to worry."

"Then what?" The sounds from the cafeteria began to fade, and I could tell she was walking somewhere more private in order to hear me better.

"I'm going to drive to California and try to get Steve Raleigh to visit Jeremy."

There was a long pause. "And to think I worried it might be something stupid."

Then I had to tell her the whole story about the genie and the wishes.

"I have to at least try to talk to Steve Raleigh," I said. "Jeremy is worried sick about the surgery."

"You can't just hop in a car and drive to California," she said.

"Yes, I can."

She let out a frustrated sigh. "Do you not have that little voice in your head that tells you when something is a bad idea?"

I dropped my curling iron into the bag, then went to the kitchen. "It's like my dad always says: When you're not winning, you have to put more effort into it. It worked for archery. It worked for volleyball. It even worked for my World History final. It will work for beating Jeremy's cancer."

There was a pause on the line. "Annika, you cheated on your World History final." That's the thing about Madison; sometimes the minor details get her off topic.

"I didn't cheat," I said. "I studied with the TA. That's different than cheating."

"He told you what was going to be on the test."

"No, he told me what *might* be on the test. We covered a lot of information. Trust me, I know way more about Sparta than I will ever use in my real life."

Even though I couldn't see it, I could tell Madison was rolling her eyes. Madison gets straight A's. In fact, she's the type that will read even more than is required on any subject. Her mind is probably filled with such vast sums of useless information it's amazing she can sort through all of it to have a normal conversation.

"Do you even know where Steve Raleigh lives?" she asked.

"I know where he works, and that's close enough. If he's not at the studio, then someone has to know how

I can contact him. Or I can snoop around the set. They've got to have his address and phone number listed in his personnel file."

"They have security guards at those places."

"I'll improvise something. You know me—I can get past anyone."

There was another pause, and then Madison's voice sounding more like a mother than a friend. "This isn't the same as getting away with stuff at school. Security guards are trained professionals. Besides, you didn't get past Mrs. Aron."

Mrs. Aron was our English teacher junior year. She assigned us oral book reports so we could practice our public speaking, but I'd been so busy with archery club and basketball finals that I didn't have time to read anything. I'd hoped she wouldn't call on me during the first day of reports, but she did, so I stood up in front of class and invented a novel. The plot, the characters, everything.

It totally ticked off Madison when Mrs. Aron gave me an A+, while Madison only received an A on a book she'd actually read. And I would have gotten away with the whole thing too, except Mrs. Aron liked my report so much she tried to find the book itself so she could read it.

After that she lowered my grade to a C: an F for the

book report, but an A+ for the public speaking part. She told me she'd raise my grade back up to an A+ if I'd write the novel and let her read it. Someday I might.

I didn't point this out to Madison, though. I dropped some apples into the duffel bag and said, "I'll find a way to get past security."

Madison's voice turned worried. "Annika, people don't just sneak off to California. Are you sure this isn't a bad reaction to stress or a nervous breakdown or something . . . ?"

I clutched the phone harder and tried to make Madison understand. "This is something I've got to do. If you can't cover for me, then let me know and I'll call someone else."

She huffed quietly to let me know she wasn't happy about it. "Fine. I'll cover for you."

After I hung up with her, I threw more food into the duffel bag. That way I wouldn't have to stop anywhere along the way. Now that I'd decided to go, it all felt urgent, as though Steve Raleigh would disappear if I didn't make it in time. I put in all the money I had. I even threw in my collection of state quarters. I tried to figure out if I would have enough money for gas and a hotel. Probably not. I'd sleep in the van and change at a fast food place.

I also packed a DVD of *Teen Robin Hood*, the first season. It would tell me the names of the people who worked on the show. Some of them had to know how to get in touch with Steve Raleigh. I went through the photo album and took out a picture of Jeremy, the one from last Halloween where he was dressed as Robin Hood. I'd show it to everyone who could help me. How could anyone say no to a sick kid who'd dressed up like Robin Hood for Halloween?

What else did I need? I looked around the room with a feeling that verged on panic. I probably needed lots of things, but I couldn't think clearly enough right now to figure out what. It was coming up on one o'clock.

Jeremy—I called his best friend's mother, Mrs. Palson, and explained that I wouldn't be home after school. Could he go home with Gabe and stay there until my parents came home?

She agreed without hesitation. Mrs. Palson dotes on Jeremy now.

Then I called my mother at work. "Hey, Mom, you know how I told you I was going over to Madison's house after school to work on that chemistry project?"

"Um . . . ," she said, and I could tell she was trying to remember the conversation that had never taken place. This is the only benefit to having your parents completely stressed out. Mom doesn't even try to keep track of what's going on in my life now.

"And Jeremy is going to the Palsons' after school," I prompted.

"Oh. Uh-huh," Mom said, pretending she knew what I was talking about.

"Well, the chemistry teacher gave us a rundown in class of everything we need to cover, and it's going to take way longer than we planned. Since it's going to be a late-nighter anyway, is it okay if I sleep over at Madison's? It's okay with Madison's parents if it's okay with you."

"On a school night?"

"Mom, the project is thirty percent of our grade."

She paused for a moment, and I worried she would come up with another objection, but instead she said, "All right, but no goofing off or staying up all night. You need your sleep."

"Thanks, Mom." After I hung up the phone, I took the Robin Hood action figure from underneath my bed and put it on my mom's pillow. If I did get caught, I wanted them to be in a good mood when they found out I wasn't at Madison's house.

Chapter 3

$\mathcal{A}$s I put on my coat, the doorbell rang. I opened the door and saw Madison standing beside a carry-on suitcase. She smiled at me as though I'd been expecting her and rolled the suitcase inside. "I decided to come with you."

I stared back at her. "What?"

She took hold of my duffel bag and swung it on top of her suitcase. "I called my mom and told her I was spending the night at your house to help you study. She couldn't say no. She knows you're having a hard time. Is this all you're bringing?"

I didn't move, even though Madison was already edging across the family room. "Madison, you can't come. If we're both gone, there's a bigger chance we'll be missed. Besides, you don't want to drive four hours to California just to stalk some TV star."

She kept walking across the family room, through

the kitchen and toward the garage. In the end, I had no choice but to follow her. She had my stuff. As she opened up the garage door, she said, "If we both go, we'll have a better chance of success. Two heads are better than one, and all that. Besides, you know you can't read a map to save your life. If you went by yourself, you'd probably end up in Mexico or something."

I took my duffel bag from off her suitcase and threw it into the back of the minivan. "I have step-by-step directions."

"I have a laptop with wireless internet. We can research Steve Raleigh as we drive. Plus, I packed a cooler with drinks, snacks, and chocolate."

I took the van keys out of my purse and didn't answer her.

"Snickers bars," she said. "And Take Fives."

"Okay, you can come."

She laughed, but it wasn't the chocolate. Madison didn't do foolish things. If she came along on the trip, somehow that meant it had a better chance of working out.

We drove to a strip-mall parking lot, where hopefully Madison's car would blend in with the folks who worked at the all-night Walgreens and remain undetected until we'd returned. This trip had to be fast. I would call the school tomorrow, pretend to be my mother, and report myself sick. I could even call Mrs. Palson again and ask her to take Jeremy after school, but I absolutely need to be home by the time my parents came home from work. We had twenty-eight hours to find Steve Raleigh and convince him to visit my brother.

I drove first while Madison stretched out in the backseat, a pillow behind her head, a bag of chips at her side, and the laptop lying across her middle. While she flipped chips into her mouth, she went to Steve Raleigh fan sites and combed through mostly pointless information. His birthday was April 9—which made him an Aries. He was nineteen years old, performed his own stunts, and owned two horses. Madison rattled it all off to me. "Did you know that besides the series, he's done two Broadway shows and three movies?" Long pause. "He started acting when he was nine. He did a toothpaste commercial."

"No wonder he has such nice teeth. They probably paid him in dental floss. Does it say anywhere that he's nice? Does he ever do charitable stuff?"

The thought of actually talking to Steve Raleigh made my stomach feel like I'd done two hundred sit-ups.

"I think he must be a nice guy because I haven't found anything bad about him yet. No rehab, no ripping up hotel rooms, no clocking his servants with cell phones. Mostly it's just that whole love triangle between him, Esme and Karli."

"He could do better than Esme," I said, as though it

audience members got to vote on. ʌ̩ry of Robin Hood is Maid Marion sup- y blond?"

ɔt ditzy in real life. She's got to be bet- ......ɪ mean, Karli dumped Steve, so I don't know why she's the one writing all those bitter love songs that everyone says are directed at him. It's like *Steve's_biggest_fan* says in her blog: Karli needs to grow up and move on with her life."

Madison's fingers tapped across the keyboard. "I'm going to leave a comment about it."

Madison also felt obligated to leave comments on a site devoted to comparing whether Esme or Karli was prettier—she voted for Karli—and left a very long comment, probably a five-paragraph essay, on someone's blog discussing whether celebrity relationships were doomed to failure. In her opinion, yes, they were.

Then she said, "Oh, here's something," and stayed quiet for an annoyingly long time while she read.

"What did you find out?" I finally asked.

"He sued his own parents. You know, it was one of those cases where he asked to be made a legal adult at sixteen. He had some sort of injunction against his parents so they couldn't spend his money. Well, that's gratitude for you. It's not like these people gave birth to you or anything."

I hoped it wasn't as bad as it sounded. How could this guy understand how I felt about my brother if he didn't care about his own family?

Madison slid the computer off her lap and leaned over the front seat. "So what are your ideas about actually tracking Steve Raleigh down? I mean, they're not going to just let us on the set to talk to him."

"We'll wait until he finishes work and follow him to wherever he goes," I said.

She shook her head. "I read on one of the blogs that the stars are chauffeured in cars with darkened windows. We'd probably end up following that fat guy who plays Friar Tuck."

"Okay. . . ." I let out a slow breath. "Plan B: we sneak onto the set."

There was a long pause from Madison. "Sneak on how? The place has got to be crawling with security guards."

"All we need to get past them is a good cover."

She let out an incredulous grunt. "A good cover? We're seventeen-year-olds. What business could we have on a set?"

"Oh, come on, a clipboard and a purposeful look will get you admitted to most places."

Madison turned and looked at me, her head tilted, sizing me up. With a slow, calculating voice she said, "I suppose you could pass for a starlet. You do have that femme fatale air about you. Like you crush boys' dreams in your spare time."

I didn't answer. I've never meant to crush anyone. And to tell you the truth, my last boyfriend, Nick, dumped me, although I know I drove him to it. Everything had been going along so well between us until Jeremy was diagnosed with cancer. In one moment, I turned from a fun girlfriend into a one-woman inquisition. Night after night, I kept asking him why God would do this. Nick had tried to come up with answers and, better yet, with consolations, but I hadn't accepted any of it. After I shredded his attempts to defend divinity, he'd finally said, "Fine, have it your way. Believe there isn't a God."

Which had made me even more indignant. "So you're saying life is some sort of cosmic accident? Everything we feel, think, and do is meaningless? If my brother dies, everything he is will just be extinguished?"

Nick had looked at me wearily, hands up like if he waited long enough he could catch some falling answers. He'd shaken his head slowly and dropped his voice to the tone of a confession.

"I can't do this anymore, Annika. I can't. Look, I'm sorry about your brother. I really am. But you don't want a shoulder to cry on, you want someone to yell at, and I'm tired of it being me."

He was right, of course, which is why I hadn't dated anyone since. I'd become broken glass. Fragile, incomplete, and cutting anyone who tried to touch me.

I could make it through school, smiling to cover up the numbness, but I couldn't make small talk with a boyfriend.

Still surveying me, Madison said, "Maybe if we make you look glamorous, the security guards will think you're a guest star."

"No. We can't be anyone important enough that people will pay attention to us. We just have to be one of the faceless workers who belong there. I'll figure something out."

After that, Madison and I switched places. She drove and I settled down in the back with the laptop. I Googled several variations of "movie set tours," trying to get a feel for what a studio would be like, what we could expect to find when we got there—and more importantly, where their security weaknesses might be. Then I tried to use the internet to find where *Teen Robin Hood* outdoor locations were, in case they were shooting there instead of the studio. The computer didn't yield any clues in that department, but I figured it couldn't be too far away from the studio. I checked aerial views of Burbank looking for open, wooded areas and wrote down the few possibilities I saw.

I put the DVD into the laptop and watched a few

minutes of an episode—mostly ignoring the story and looking at the background. The sheriff's men rode horses over hills, and there was also a river. I hadn't seen a river anywhere near the studio. Had the TV show makers faked the river? Was that possible? I'd just have to hope the cast was working at the set right now—either that or that the locals knew where the outdoor location was.

My attention, however, kept leaving the background and resting on Robin Hood. Well, how could I help staring at him? They had all those close-up shots. Shots that showed his square jaw, penetrating brown eyes, and impossible smirk. His hair hung to his shoulders in messy blond waves, and he even made that ridiculous feathered hat look good.

He moved effortlessly, frozen in time and space on the laptop, but he was really out there somewhere right now. I wondered what he was doing this very instant.

Eventually I tore my attention away from his grin, skipped to the end of the episode, and wrote down all the names of the people it listed working on the set. From the director, Dean Powell, all the way down to the best boy—I had no idea what that actually was. Ditto for the gaffer. I always thought a gaffer was a really old guy, but apparently not.

I had hoped to memorize some of the names so when I got to the set I'd seem like someone who belonged, but the sheer number of them overwhelmed me. What did all of these people do? You could invade a country with fewer people.

I ran an internet search on Dean Powell so I'd be able to recognize him if I saw him. I came up with an interview and a picture of a man who, despite his casual attire and shoulder-length hair, still managed to seem stern, temperamental, and not at all like the sort who would appreciate two teenage girls sneaking onto his set. I didn't share this impression with Madison, though.

As I studied studio links, another thing became apparent: Movie people had a language all their own. I repeated the vocabulary out loud: *dailies, dolly, dubbing, dunning* . . . committing the words to memory in a way that would have amazed my Spanish teacher.

At the same time, I sifted through ideas to get onto the set. I could pretend to be a reporter from a teen magazine or perhaps someone delivering something for wardrobe, maybe an agent's assistant. I shut my eyes trying to consider all the possibilities. The hum of the wheels mixed in with my thoughts, turning and turning, and the next thing I knew it was five-thirty and Madison had pulled into a gas station in Burbank. The studio was just down the road.

While Madison filled up the car, I walked into the convenience store and bought drinks. I stood at the cash register, still trying to shake off the last dull feelings of sleep, and eyed over the elderly clerk. I could tell he was lonely.

Sometimes being able to read people makes me sad. At first it upset me to realize how many people are, at heart, selfish. Now I take that in stride, but people's loneliness still gets to me.

I knew he wouldn't mind talking to me, though. All I'd have to do was ask and he would tell me everything he knew about the studio.

Trying to sound like a tourist, I asked, "Do they give tours of that studio down the street?"

He shook his head. "Not when they're shooting the series. You could check with them in the summer, though."

It hadn't even occurred to me that they might not be filming now, and I breathed a sigh of relief. What would I have done if they'd been on hiatus?

I fingered the gum sitting by the register as though trying to decide on a flavor. "They're filming right now, this very minute?"

"Nah, I'm sure they're done for the day. They always quit early when the Lakers have a basketball game, what with Mr. Powell being a big fan, and all." He took the pack of gum from my hands and ran it across the scanner. "The studio even has its own box at the sports arena. A luxury suite. One of the perks of fame."

I handed him my money. "They all go up there?"

He opened the register and nodded. *"Entertainment Tonight* is always reporting on who took who there. That guy who plays Robin Hood is a regular."

"Really?" The word came out of my mouth too eager, and the man chuckled at me.

"Yeah, the young ones always go for him. The older ladies take a liking to the Sheriff of Nottingham." He gave me the change. "I should have been an actor. Think of the money I wasted on cologne, when all along I just had to spout something off on TV with an English accent."

He would have said more, but I'd picked up my stuff and was already moving to the door. "Thanks," I called back, then hurried across the parking lot to the van.

It meant we didn't have to wait until tomorrow. We could try and find him tonight. The thought made me feel both nervous and keyed up. I could hardly sit still. Could I do this? I had to, didn't I? Why else had I come all this way?

While we ate a rushed dinner, I used MapQuest to get directions for the Staples Sports Center in LA.

"It's worth a try," I said, my mind clicking through options, processing a plan.

"Where are we going to get tickets?" Madison asked. "I didn't bring a lot of money."

I popped a piece of sandwich into my mouth and didn't answer.

Madison lowered the apple she was eating, her face

tense. She sent me an incredulous look. "You want to sneak into the game, don't you?"

"No. We'll wait until after halftime to show up. By that time security isn't so tight."

Madison relaxed enough to take another bite of her apple. "Okay, that might work."

"Of course, we'll still have to sneak into the box."

She gripped her apple. "My stomach suddenly hurts."

"You said you wanted to come with me," I reminded her.

"Yeah, because I thought I could stop you from doing something stupid. I'm beginning to wonder if that's possible."

I fingered the crust of my sandwich and didn't say anything. It did seem stupid, but what did it matter if it didn't work? We wouldn't be any worse off than we were now. And it might work. Really, all of that positive thinking stuff I've read must be having an effect on me.

I smiled at Madison to show her I was confident. "It will be fine. We'll just need to stop at a thrift shop first and see if we can pick up something that looks like a uniform. Maybe some smocks or vests." I grabbed the laptop again and went back to the MapQuest site.

She didn't stop clutching her apple. "You know, all of this subterfuge is bad karma. It will come back to bite you someday. And even if it doesn't," she said, anticipating my total lack of worry in the karma department, "our parents will kill us if we get arrested."

"We're not going to get arrested. God owes me that much."

Madison scooted over and looked at the computer screen, where I'd pulled up a listing of secondhand stores. "I thought you didn't believe in God anymore."

"I never said that. I said I wasn't speaking to him anymore."

Madison let out a sigh. "Oh, great. We're about to do something risky, and you're going to tick off God beforehand." Madison turned her face upward and called, "She doesn't mean it."

I rolled my eyes.

"Don't look at me like that," she said. "When you're in jail and I'm not, we'll see who's rolling their eyes."

I handed Madison the laptop and started the van. "There's a Goodwill a couple miles away."

Chapter 4

The problem with internet directions is that they're not always clear. That is the only reason it took us half an hour to get to the store and not, as Madison claimed, because I drive too fast, pass by streets, and then recklessly make U-turns in the middle of four lanes of traffic. But we got there safely which, I told Madison, proved I had not ticked off God after all.

We bought a couple pairs of black pants and white buttoned-down shirts, which is pretty much a typical waiter uniform. Then we went to a beauty supply store for the crowning touch: hairnets. Hairnets scream food service, because no sane person would wear them otherwise. We changed at a McDonald's, drove to LA, and made it to the Staples Center as halftime ended.

I put money, keys, and my picture of Jeremy into my pocket, then we shoved our purses underneath the seats to discourage thieves. We couldn't carry anything with us, because we had to look like we were working at one of the food booths.

We hurried across the parking lot and strode into the building. None of the ushers questioned us. That part, at least, couldn't have been easier. We weaved in and out of the crowds who were returning to their seats, until we found a food booth. I bought two bags of popcorn, three hot dogs, a pretzel, and six drinks. They gave us a flat to carry the drinks in, but it was still enough food that both our hands were full. That was the important thing.

As we walked away, I told Madison, "Now we've just got to find the right box."

We would know it was the right one because any box the stars frequented would have a security guard by the entrance. The plan was to walk up and say that Mr. Raleigh had ordered the food. The security guard would either look at us oddly and say "Who's Mr. Raleigh?" or he'd let us go up.

We walked around the stadium, past security guards standing and milling around, but I didn't see anyone guarding the stairwell entrances or the elevators. I began to think I'd guessed wrong. Maybe the security guards were on the other side of the door. Maybe none of the cast of *Robin Hood* had come to the game this time. Maybe the guy at the gas station was just spinning tales to impress the tourists.

And then I saw him. A guy so big he belonged on a football field. He wore an earpiece and a serious look. His hands were folded in front of him like a neon ON DUTY sign. Standing next to the elevator door, he reminded me of a bull in a pasture. I could tell right away he wasn't just a security guard, he was actually guarding something.

"This is it," I whispered to Madison. "Remember to look the part." My pace slowed involuntarily. I had to force myself to keep taking steps in the guy's direction. I tried to appear confident.

I walked up to the man, nodding. "Hey, this is the food Mr. Raleigh ordered. You want to hit the elevator button for me? My hands are full."

He gave me an unimpressed stare. "You got a pass?"

I jutted my hip out and rested the drinks on it. "No, but I got real sore feet. Are you going to get the button for me?"

"Can't let anyone through without a VIP pass, but I'll call someone to come down and get this stuff." He reached for a button on his earpiece.

I adjusted the tray on my hip, moving it further away from him. "I can't just give the food away. It hasn't been paid for yet."

Now the guy's eyes narrowed. "Didn't they put it on their account?"

"Oh, right. Their account." I knew I'd been beaten,

but I tried one last time. "Look, would it really be a big deal to let us deliver it? I've never been up to a luxury suite."

He shrugged dismissively. "Sorry. Without a pass I couldn't let my mother up there. Someone will be here in a minute."

And so we waited, trapped by our lie. Madison stood at my side, shivering enough that every once in a while a piece of popcorn fell out of her container onto the ground. I wondered if whoever came down would know we were lying and would yell at us or turn us in. But then again, maybe it would be Steve Raleigh.

The doors might open and I'd see his shaggy blond hair and arrogant smile. Maybe he'd even say something in that irresistible English accent. Oh, wait, the accent was probably fake. I tried to imagine Steve Raleigh sounding like an American, but only for a moment. I had to think of something to say to him. How does one throw herself at someone's mercy while delivering soda?

Finally, the elevator door opened and a guy I didn't recognize stepped out. A cord with a pale blue name tag that read BALLARD PRODUCTIONS dangled around his neck. Just a simple blue piece of paper was keeping me down here.

The guy looked over at the food. "Man, they've got prime rib upstairs and somebody ordered hot dogs?" He shook his head. "That's how you know you're overfeeding the talent—when they're sick of prime rib."

He held out his hands for my tray, and I grudgingly handed it to him. Altogether it had cost forty-five dollars. Stadium food is way overpriced. Not only had I blown the money, I wouldn't even be able to eat any of it.

The guy glanced over at Madison. "I'll have to make two trips to get this."

"That's fine," she said. Her voice came out as a croak. The elevator door shut, and we all stood silently staring at one another.

The guard asked, "Do you guys need to get back to work?" and he held out his hands for the popcorn.

Madison glanced at me. "I guess we'd better."

I nodded, and she handed over the food. We took slow steps away from the elevator. Madison whispered, "We were so close."

Yes, so close. If I could just talk to Steve Raleigh, if I could explain. . . .

I looked over my shoulder at the security guard. He wasn't watching us anymore—in fact, he was eating some of the popcorn. I took a few more steps away to make sure he couldn't hear us talk. "Do you think there's any way we could forge one of those VIP passes?"

"Not really," she said.

I looked beyond her, my gaze drifting in the direction of the bleachers. "It would take some time. We'd have to find an office store that sells light blue paper and those name tag holders, then we'd have to get access to a computer printer with the right font. I'd also need to totally change my appearance. How much time do you suppose is left in the game?"

She didn't answer, but it didn't matter because right then I noticed a guy walking in our direction. He was tall, probably six-two, and wore a Lakers team jacket and ski cap so only wisps of brown hair showed across his forehead. Black-rim glasses perched above his nose, which gave him the look of a jock trying to pass himself off as an intellectual.

He was good-looking enough that I automatically cringed inside. I'd randomly shoved all my hair into a hairnet, which undoubtedly made me look like an angry blond beaver was attacking my head. He was that handsome—but the most striking thing about him was the blue Ballard Productions pass that hung around his neck.

I wanted it.

I gazed at his dark brown eyes, trying to calculate his personality as he came toward me. It's hard to do this with really attractive people because sometimes I get caught up in who I want them to be instead of who they are. This guy definitely made it hard to concentrate, but he did have a familiar feel to him. Like an old friend. I could tell he was a decent sort of guy, one who would stop to help someone stuck on the side of a road. And I was about as stuck as I could get.

I took several steps toward him so I intercepted him before he got within earshot of the security guard.

"Are you going up to the box?" I asked him.

He glanced at me, surprised. "Yeah."

"You work for the TV studio?"

He shrugged. "When I have to."

My gaze went back to the pass lying against his jacket. I couldn't think of how to best ask him, so I blurted out, "This will seem like a strange request, but I have a perfectly legitimate reason for asking. Can I borrow your pass for a few minutes?"

Madison had joined me by this time but didn't say anything. She kept casting nervous glances back at the security guard.

An intrigued look passed over the guy's face. "And what's your perfectly legitimate reason?"

I hesitated, not sure how much of the truth I should tell him. I lowered my voice. "I need to talk to Steve Raleigh."

"Really?" The guy cocked his head, an amused smile on his lips. "What are you: fans, writers or . . ." His eyes traveled over our black pants, white shirts, and hairnets. "I'm guessing hopeful actresses." He made a move as if to walk past us. "Sorry, Steve doesn't have anything to do with casting."

"Wait." I stepped into his path so he couldn't get around me. "That's not it. I'm just a fan. A huge fan, really, and I have this favor I need to ask him—it's a charity thing, but it would be good publicity for him too, and—"

He held up a hand to cut me off. "You're a huge fan?" He eyed me over, clearly doubtful.

"Yes." To prove it I added, "I can tell you he performs most of his own stunts." That had been one of the facts Madison had recited to me. "He's done two Broadway shows and three movies." I rattled off the titles, even though I'd never seen any of them. Then I picked two more facts I could remember off the top of my head. "He owns a couple horses, and he did his first commercial when he was nine years old. A toothpaste commercial. They paid him in dental floss. Well, not really—I made up the last part, but the rest of it's true. So you can see I'm a huge fan. Can I please borrow your pass?"

He looked up, thinking, then returned his gaze to my face. "How about we make a deal? I'll ask you a Steve Raleigh trivia question. If you can answer it correctly, I'll stay down here and let you borrow my pass so you can go up to the box."

"Okay." Eagerness itched inside of me, and I nearly bounced on the balls of my feet. A part of my mind was already racing ahead to plan out the next step. I'd have to change into something else so the guard wouldn't recognize me. Putting on my normal clothes probably wouldn't be enough. Could I get a hold of some sunglasses? A hat?

"Here's the question," the guy said. "What does Steve Raleigh look like in real life?"

I hesitated because it was such an obvious question. "He has . . ." I meant to say blond hair, but suddenly I wasn't sure. I'd just assumed it was blond because that's how I'd seen him in *Robin Hood*. But in one of the pictures I'd seen in my internet search, he'd had shoulder-length black hair and a mustache—that had been when he'd had a part of a gunslinger in a Western. And he did have brown eyes. But in the pictures of him from that Civil War movie, he'd had blond hair. Ditto for the Viking flick. On his website they'd had photos of him as Robin Hood, photos from his movies, and one of him sitting in a chair holding a guitar—he had brown hair in that one, but I'd figured that was a photo from one of his plays.

Suddenly I wished I'd done more research. Madison had been the one going to all the internet sites about him. I'd spent my time during the road trip memorizing names off the DVD, learning movie lingo, studying sets, and trying to find the outside location.

I glanced at Madison for help, but she was gazing wide-eyed at the guy and not looking at me at all.

Since the guy was waiting for me to finish my sentence, I stammered out, "He has . . . brown eyes."

The guy stared at me silently, waiting for me to say more. A smile tugged at the corners of his mouth. Madison let out a sound that was half gasp, like I'd said the wrong thing, which annoyed me since he did have brown eyes. Unless he wore contacts in the Robin Hood series. I decided not to consider that possibility, and I went on, ignoring the whole hair question. "And he's tall, and has this chiseled jaw—"

Madison gasped again. I wasn't sure why. I knew I had that part right.

"And he's in good shape. He has, um, really nice arm muscles, and—"

"Blond or brown hair?" the guy asked me.

I glanced at Madison again. She was still staring at the guy, her mouth half open like she was going to say something, but she didn't. I decided to guess. It looked so good blond; it must be his natural color. "Blond," I said.

He shrugged and gave me a conciliatory smile. "Sorry, you failed the huge-fan test. It's actually brown." He pushed past us before I could protest or think of anything else to say.

I watched him go, with a "But . . ." hovering on my lips. Before he'd gotten more than a few steps away, the security guard approached us. He grunted at Madison and me, then turned his gaze to the guy.

"I hope these girls aren't bothering you, Mr. Raleigh."

The guy sent us another smile—the same arrogant smirk, I now realized, I'd seen time and time again on *Teen Robin Hood*. "No, we were just talking. They're huge fans of mine."

And with a very Robin-Hood-like nod in our direction, he disappeared into the elevator.

Chapter 5

Madison lay on one of the beds in our motel room, and I lay on the other. I had suggested sleeping in the van because we'd already spent most of our cash, but Madison had brought her parents' credit card with her. They gave it to her to use in emergencies, and she figured having to sleep in a van in a parking lot in California constituted an emergency. By the time her parents noticed the charge, we'd be home to explain it.

Still, we'd gone to the cheapest motel in LA we could find. The walls were dirty, the carpet was matted, and the sheets were so worn and thin you could have used them for tracing paper.

It was late, but I couldn't bring myself to get in my pajamas or brush my teeth. I lay there fully dressed staring at the ceiling. I wished I could have a good, long crying jag, but for some reason I can't cry.

My mom cries. She cries a lot now. You can say something perfectly normal like "Have you seen my math homework?" and she will burst into tears and rush into her room. It is no use trying to comfort her. She has to get it out of her system before she can emerge and be upbeat again.

Leah is an expert at crying. I have seen her weep when Mom and Dad yelled at her, and then stop as soon as they left the room. And I'm not talking about whining, which anyone can do, I'm talking actual tears dripping down her cheeks.

As kids, whenever we got into fights and my parents heard her sobbing side of the story and then my clear-eyed one, I always got into trouble. So I definitely see the benefit of crying. It's just when something goes wrong in my life and I'm overwhelmed by frustration, there is a moment where I teeter between anger and tears. I can feel it, but somehow my emotions always slide toward anger.

I didn't really want to cry as I lay there thinking about my meeting with Steve Raleigh. I wanted to scream, loudly and repeatedly. But I couldn't. That's a thing about our society; we totally understand when a person breaks down and cries, but if the same person were to scream at the top of her lungs in a motel room, it is fairly certain the other guests would flee from the building and the hotel manager would call the police.

"If you thought it was him," I said to Madison for the third time, "why didn't you say something? Why didn't you stop me?"

For the third time, she answered me patiently. She sat on the edge of her bed coating her legs with lotion and hardly looked at me. "Because I wasn't sure, and wouldn't we have looked even stupider if halfway through his quiz I'd said, 'Hey, aren't *you* Steve Raleigh?' and it turned out it wasn't him? Besides," she added more quietly, "when I realized it might be him, I lost all ability to actually speak."

I spread my fingers against the stale bedspread. Instead of being soft, it felt vaguely like wax paper. "Well, I'd rather look stupid in front of a guy who turned out *not* to be Steve Raleigh than one who turned out to be him."

She finished up her legs and began spreading lotion on her arms. "I still can't believe it was *him*. Steve Raleigh. Standing right in front of us. He *spoke* to us."

"Yeah. And we made fools of ourselves." I winced as I said this. It hurt to remember it.

"Yeah, but we made fools of ourselves in front of *Steve Raleigh*," she said dreamily. "I didn't think he'd be so good-looking in real life, did you?"

"I obviously didn't give a lot of thought to what he looked like in real life, or I would have recognized him—but you, Madison, you saw all those pictures of him on the internet, why didn't you say something?"

She set the lotion bottle down with a thud, and her voice took on a sharp edge. "Yeah, because that way he would have given you his pass so you could go up to the box—where he clearly wasn't. We were doomed as soon as you talked to him without knowing who he was."

She was right. I should have recognized him. Hair color, hat, and glasses aside, I'd seen him enough times as Robin Hood that I should have known who he was. But one doesn't expect to see celebrities, unannounced and wearing normal clothes—suddenly there—in the ordinary world. Besides, I'd been concentrating so hard on getting a pass, I'd been so busy figuring out the next step of my plan, my mind just hadn't processed what it should have.

I pulled myself over to the side of the bed and put my hand to my temple. "I'm sorry, Madison. I know it was my fault, not yours. I should have known it was him, and I should have made it clear it was my little brother who was the huge fan."

Silence filled the room, and I wasn't sure if Madison accepted my olive branch or not. After a moment, she turned so she could see me better and her voice softened. "Even if you had, it might not have turned out differently. He didn't seem all that interested in doing anybody any favors." She pulled back the covers and slid under them. "At least we can say we tried. Think of it this way, you'll have a really funny story to tell your brother about how we met Steve Raleigh."

Only Jeremy wouldn't think it was funny. I couldn't go home and tell him I'd lied about everything and there wasn't really a genie to help him make it through surgery. I just couldn't.

I turned over on my back and stared at the ceiling again. "I've got to try one more time to see him. We'll go to the set tomorrow and try to talk to him there."

Doubt flashed across Madison's face. "Annika, it was a miracle we saw him tonight. How are we going to get into the set?"

How, yes. It was time to decide on that. I thought back to the website about all the lingo TV people used, letting it stream through my mind. It seemed they had a different name for everything. They didn't even call caterers *caterers*. They were *food craft*. But they probably all wore some sort of uniform. Who had access to the place that wouldn't be in uniform? And then I thought of it.

"We'll have to find a pet store before we drive to the set," I told Madison. "We'll be animal wranglers. That will get us past the security guards. Once we're on the set, we'll—"

"If Steve Raleigh didn't want to help us tonight," Madison said, breaking into my thoughts, "what makes you think he'd want to help us tomorrow?"

"We never got a chance to explain anything to him. If I could talk to him, I could convince him to visit Jeremy. Besides," I propped myself up on my elbows, "we were wearing food service uniforms and our hair was shoved into hairnets. I'd be willing to bet he won't be any better at recognizing us than we were at recognizing him." I held up a strand of my long blond hair. "How do you think I'd look as a brunette?"

Madison held up her hands in protest. "Oh, no—I'm not dyeing my hair. Don't even ask."

"You can change it back afterward," I said. "Let's go to the store right now. Do you want to be a brunette, platinum blond—or you could try jet black."

"I'm tired," she said. "I'm not going anywhere tonight but across the room to turn off the light."

I conceded that part to her. The nice thing about Madison is that as long as I let her win some of the battles, she lets me win the war. I changed into my pajamas, climbed into bed, and tried to go over all of the details in my mind so I'd be prepared for anything tomorrow.

After a few hours of listening to the room's heater turn on and off, I eventually fell asleep. My mind returned to my neighborhood: to rows of pale stucco houses, to cactus and palm trees, to little oasis circles of grass growing among sun-bleached rock yards, to all things average, familiar, and comforting. I was in my living room now, its usual clutter surrounding me, lulling me with a feeling of security.

And then I looked out the window and saw the Grim Reaper.

He walked down our road, turning his long, hooded head from one house to the other, searching. He seemed to glide effortlessly, and yet each footstep hit the pavement with the sound of cracking ice. Fear exploded in my chest, and I yelled for Jeremy to hide. I ran outside, locking the door behind me. I couldn't find a weapon and didn't have time to go back inside for my bow and arrows, so I picked up a shovel. I walked toward the robed figure, holding the shovel out in front of me with shaking hands.

"Pass by our house," I told him. "I won't let you come in."

He stopped and leaned on his scythe, long insectlike fingers clutching it for support. I couldn't see his face, just a black opening under his hood, but I could tell he was considering me. Then, his dark face turned from mine and gazed past me to our house. He straightened up as though about to walk in that direction.

"Take me instead," I said. My voice was no more than a gasped whisper, but I knew he'd heard me.

He shook his head slowly, and when he spoke, his

voice, hollow and grating, left the air around me cold. "Do you think I deal in years or decades? You'll be with me soon enough. I don't need to make bargains with your kind."

He moved as if to go on, but before he could pass me, I swung my shovel and knocked the scythe out of his hand. It tumbled to the street with the rattle of endless chains.

I went to grab it, but it jumped away from me and flew back into the hands of its master.

"You haven't the power to defeat me," he said.

"Then I'll delay you."

But I couldn't. He walked right through me and then was beyond me, gliding toward my house.

My heart pounded so hard it seemed to catapult from one side of my chest to the other. "No!" I yelled.

The Grim Reaper disappeared, and I found myself sitting up in the motel bed.

Madison clumsily reached for the light between us. "What's wrong?"

I put my hand over my eyes to shield my face from the light. "Nothing. What time is it?"

"It's three-thirty. Did you have a nightmare?"

I blinked, trying to locate my cell phone among the scattered contents on the nightstand. The frustration made my hands feel clumsy. Even though the light was on, even though I knew it had only been a dream, the feeling of panic hadn't left me. "I think I should call home to see if Jeremy is okay."

"At three-thirty in the morning?"

"I just . . . I think I should check to make sure all the doors are locked."

She rubbed one hand over her eyes. "Annika, you want to wake up everyone in your family to ask about the doors? Who are you afraid is going to break in?"

I couldn't find my cell phone on the nightstand, and I picked up my purse to check there. My voice came out too fast. "Anyone. The Grim Reaper, maybe. You should just always make sure your doors are locked."

She looked at me silently, her eyes trying to adjust to both the light and my logic. She could have said the obvious, which was "Are you insane?" or something a little less obvious but still to the point, like "I don't think the Grim Reaper uses the front door. He goes down the chimney like Santa Claus."

Instead she said "Oh, Annika," climbed out of bed, and walked to the dresser. She sifted through its contents until she retrieved my cell phone, then came back and handed it to me. "Call if it will make you feel better."

I looked at the phone in my hand, but put it on the nightstand. "I can't call. They'd tell me to come home, and I'm four hours away. I'll call him in the morning."

She nodded and climbed back into her bed. "He's going to be all right."

"I know," I said.

She turned off the light, and I reached over and took my cell phone from the nightstand. I laid it against my cheek on my pillow and shut my eyes, even though I knew I wouldn't be able to go back to sleep.

In the morning, we ate most of our stock of food, then drove to a drugstore for hair dye. Madison didn't say anything about our conversation from the middle of the night. She didn't even comment when I called Jeremy before school and told him a story about a sister who loved her little brother so much she went to the underworld to retrieve him. Usually I tell Jeremy stories about a heroic little boy, but today I needed the sister to be the hero.

"It's supposed to be about a mother and a daughter," Jeremy told me. "You know, Persephone."

Jeremy always says her name Purse-n-phone, probably because that's the way my dad first pronounced it when he read the story to him. No amount of my insisting that it's pronounced Per-se-fon-ee has made a dent in either Dad's or Jeremy's pronunciation. I became eternally grateful when Jeremy stopped idolizing Hercules and we no longer had to listen to Dad's butchered versions of Greek and Roman names.

"This is a different story," I told Jeremy. "In this one, a sister and brother were out playing catch by their house. They lived by a cliff and their parents had told them not to play near the edge, but on this day they didn't listen."

"What's the sister's name?" he asked.

"What do you want her to be named?"

"Annie," he said. "And the brother's name is Jeremy."

I hesitated. I didn't want to use his name for this story, as if even connecting his name with the under-world would endanger him.

He didn't wait for me to come up with a logical rea-son to protest this decision, though. "So Jeremy and Annie were out playing," he prompted. "And then what happened?"

"Well, the little brother ran to catch the ball, and he fell off the edge of the cliff all the way down to the un-derworld. In fact, when Hades first found him, Jeremy was trying to retrieve the ball from Cerberus, the three-headed dog. You know how dogs are. They love to play catch. One head had the ball, and the other two heads wouldn't stop licking Jeremy's face."

Jeremy laughed but didn't comment, so I went on. "Jeremy's family missed him in the worst way, so Annie decided she had to go after him and bring him back."

"How did she get to the underworld?" Jeremy asked.

"She cried so hard her tears formed a river, and tears

of grief always run into the river Styx. She simply followed their trail there. Well, of course, Hades didn't want to let Jeremy go. Hades has a no-leaving policy when it comes to the underworld. But Annie walked right up to Hades and explained that she had to take Jeremy with her."

"What did Hades say?"

In my mind I tried to picture the cartoon character of Hades from Disney's *Hercules* movie. I meant to answer in his voice, complete with New York accent. But I couldn't picture him. I saw only the Grim Reaper from my dream, with his empty, dark face. I saw him so clearly it made me catch my breath, and a wave of anxiety swept over me. He stood on the highest precipice in an endless cavern of gray, one never pierced by sunlight.

Since I didn't answer, Jeremy went on. "Did Hades fall in love with Annie because she was so beautiful?"

"No, the Grim Reaper has no heart, so he doesn't care how beautiful a girl is."

"The Grim Reaper?" Jeremy repeated. "I thought it was Hades."

"The Grim Reaper is just another one of his names," I said.

"So how did Annie rescue her brother?"

I had meant to tell him she cut off all her hair, wove it into a rope, and used her bow and arrow to shoot the rope of hair to the edge of the underworld. Then they both climbed up together. But the vision of the gray cavern was too strong in my mind. I could still see it, and there was no edge.

"She cut off all of her hair," I said.

The Grim Reaper turned an icy stare in my direction. "It won't work."

"And she braided it into a rope, like in the story of Rapunzel."

The Reaper's hollow voice echoed toward me. "It's impossible."

"Then she used her bow and arrow to shoot the rope to the very edge of the underworld."

I must not have sounded convincing because Jeremy let out a "nu-uh" of disbelief. "Your hair isn't that long," he said.

"It grew during the walk to the underworld."

"Isn't the underworld a long way down?"

Apparently that ending wasn't going to satisfy him. In the background, I heard my father calling Jeremy's name.

"I'm not finished with the story," I said. "When the arrow flew away, she saw the rope wouldn't be long enough. But she took Jeremy's hand and told him they'd figure out a way to escape from the underworld together."

My father's voice became louder, and I knew he stood

near Jeremy. "Come on, buddy," I heard him say. "It's time to go."

Jeremy said, "But Annika's telling me a story."

"She can finish it later. The school bus is coming." Next my father's voice came on the line. "Shouldn't you be in class?"

"I'm taking a break." Which, technically, was true.

He didn't question me about it. Instead he let his voice drop to a whisper and added, "Thanks for the you-know-what you left on our bed. You-know-who is going to love it."

"Don't make him wait for Christmas to open it," I said. "You can let him have it whenever."

"Maybe later tonight," he said. "Now you'd better get back to class."

I hung up with him, called in sick to the school, then phoned Mrs. Palson and asked her to pick up Jeremy from school again. I had until one o'clock—well, one-thirty if I drove fast—until I had to leave for Nevada.

It took a good part of the morning to dye our hair. Madison and I both went medium golden brown. She bought the temporary kind that washes out after a few shampoos, but I went for the permanent. Part of me wanted a permanent change—as though if I changed my hair color, I could leave everything behind.

Madison fussed over her hair, but I liked mine. It made my blue eyes seem darker, more mysterious. I curled my hair so it was wavy and voluptuous. I flipped it around so it fell in my face, then I gave the mirror sultry looks. This, I thought, must be how Leah feels all of the time.

Madison stood behind me, applying foundation, but watching me. "I thought you were going to be an animal wrangler, not a starlet."

"I am an animal wrangler. I'm just one with starlet potential."

Madison steadied her face for mascara and blinked. "I can't believe I'm doing this."

"I can't believe you are either." I left my hair alone and picked up my eye-shadow compact. "Although I notice neither one of us said we couldn't believe *I'm* doing this."

She laughed but didn't comment. Sometimes I wonder if I'm a bad influence on Madison.

We found a pet store and then had to wait until ten o'clock, when it opened. Using Madison's credit card, we bought a cage full of rabbits and an aquarium with a five-foot Burmese python. I purposely chose a snake because enough people didn't like them that if I was, say, walking across the studio lot with a large one draped across my arm, people might stay away from me.

The lady at the pet store assured me the snake— Herman, she called him—was a sweetheart and not at all venomous. She took him out of his tank and hung him around her neck like a feather boa just to prove the point. He held his head up, surveying me with piercing black eyes, and licked the air. Then the lady put the snake around my neck and I felt the muscles in his body pulse as his smooth skin slid over mine.

"Oh, yes," I said in a voice several degrees higher than my normal one. "I can tell he's a sweetheart. I'll take him."

I was able to make it back to the van before I started shuddering uncontrollably.

Besides the rabbits and snake, we bought a couple of doves in a large wire cage so our van would look convincingly like one belonging to a pair of animal wranglers. It was a good idea, except that both doves and all the rabbits had apparently picked up on the fact that a large carnivorous snake rode in the van with them. As I drove, the rabbits bounced about their cage, alternately running into each other and the walls, while every so often the doves would flap their wings in a frenzy. It was nearly as distracting as Madison gripping her door handle and hissing, "Would you please slow down?"

Almost as if in answer to her wish, we hit construction coming into Burbank and progressed through town at a crawling pace. It was almost eleven when we pulled into the road that led to the studio. I grabbed my dad's old baseball cap from underneath the seat and put it on my head in hopes it would somehow make me look older, or at least less recognizable. Then I leaned back in my seat and draped one hand casually across the steering wheel as we pulled up to the guard booth. A middle-aged man in a white uniform looked at me with the same expression a cat gives you when you've disturbed his nap.

I smiled up at him. "Hi, I'm dropping off animals for the shoot."

He gazed down at the cages, and the doves made an impressive attempt for freedom by trying to fly through their food dish. I heard birdseed scattering across the van.

"Where's your pass?" the guard asked.

I looked around as though I'd misplaced it. "I know I brought it. . . . I remember having it in my hand. . . ." I flipped through pieces of paper on the seat between Madison and me, then flipped through them again. "Do you think it's under one of the cages?"

Madison shrugged. "It could be."

I turned back to the guard. "This might take a minute. I'm going to need to pick up all of the cages. Could you maybe help me out and grab the snake for a minute?"

Madison let out an impatient groan. "We can't be late. You know how Mr. Powell gets when he has to wait."

"It won't take long," I told her.

She held up both hands. "Fine, but he's not yelling at me. You can tell him you had to play show-and-tell with the security guard."

The guard let out a sigh and waved us through. I had to suppress a shriek of joy as we drove past him. We were inside.

Chapter 6

We parked outside of the studio. I took my cell phone and Jeremy's Robin Hood picture from my purse, slipped them into my jeans pocket, then shoved my purse underneath the seat.

I hefted the snake aquarium out of the van. "Now we just have to find Steve Raleigh's trailer."

Madison nodded, but as we walked around the building, she kept casting nervous glances behind her.

We hadn't gone far before the aquarium grew really heavy. I shifted its weight, trying to get a better grip. "Do you suppose he has his own trailer?"

"I have no idea."

"That's the thing about the internet. It's really good at giving you pointless facts like how many horses a star owns, but not important things like how to invade his trailer."

Madison eyed me suspiciously. "When you say

'invade,' you actually mean 'knock on the door,' right? You're not going to pick the lock or anything, are you?"

"Picking locks is very hard. I prefer climbing through windows."

She let out a grunt, so I added, "Don't be so uptight. Hollywood is used to people trying to break into the business."

"That is not what the saying means, and you know it."

We turned the building's corner. Instead of trailers, a huge canopy that covered rows of tables spread out before us. Even from far away, I could smell the food. The aroma of something spicy and warm floated up to me.

Dozens of people sat at the tables eating. More people mingled in front of the buffet tables. It was odd to see people decked out in medieval costume sitting next to others wearing jeans and sweatshirts.

Automatically my eyes searched for Robin Hood's trademark hat. I didn't see it. Several of the Sheriff of Nottingham's men, complete with costumes, sat together eating, but Steve wasn't with them. I also saw a burly guy wearing a navy blue policemanlike shirt. A security guard.

I shifted the aquarium's weight onto my hip and said, "Maybe Steve hasn't come to eat yet."

"You know," Madison said, "maybe the big stars eat in their trailers. I don't see any of them out here."

We only had a couple of hours to find him, hope he didn't recognize us as the idiots from last night, and figure out a way to talk to him. Lunch would be perfect for that, but who knew what his schedule was like. If he ate lunch in his trailer, we'd waste a lot of time waiting around for him.

And I couldn't afford to waste any time.

I also couldn't take Herman with me to the buffet. I was fairly certain real animal wranglers didn't do that.

"I think we should split up," I said.

Madison let out a squeaky protest, and I hurried on before she could speak. "You hang out at the lunch tables. Eat things. That's not so hard; if anyone asks, tell them you work on props. Stay until they either kick you out or I come back. If Steve Raleigh shows up, sit by him—and I don't care how many burly Merry Men you have to push out of the way to do it. Talk to him. Explain the situation."

She nodded. "What are you going to do?"

"I'm going to look for his trailer . . . check out the studio building. . . ." It sounded pathetic even to my own ears, and I looked upward. "If God loves me at all, I'll run into Steve Raleigh in the break room." I wasn't sure if studios even had break rooms. This was another way the internet had failed me. Still looking up, I added, "That's not too much of a miracle to ask for, is it? I just want five minutes by a soda machine."

Madison put her hand on my arm, and her voice took on that soothing tone she uses when she's concerned about me. "Maybe it isn't wise to judge God's love by Steve Raleigh's break room habits."

I looked down at Herman, who was now trying to scale the walls of the aquarium. He probably didn't like being jostled. "Wish me luck," I said, then turned and walked away from the buffet area before I could change my mind.

I continued on my trek around the studio, and this time when I rounded the corner, I saw a row of trailers flanking the building.

At least a dozen large Winnebagos stretched in a line across the pavement. I headed toward them, looking for a clue as to which belonged to Steve Raleigh. It would have been nice if there had been names on the doors, but there weren't. I walked by the front of the trailers, hoping to hear something from one of them. Perhaps Steve's voice. I didn't hear anything, though.

By the time I'd reached the end of the trailer row— there were fourteen of them—my arm muscles burned with the strain of carrying the aquarium and my hands stung. Herman kept watching me with disapproving eyes. You wouldn't think snakes could glare, but trust me, they can.

Past the trailers I could see a corral with horses. The faint sound of hooves and whinnies drifted over the lot.

I needed to stay away from there so I wouldn't run into any of the actual animal wranglers.

I rested the aquarium against my hip and looked back at the trailers. Which trailer was Steve's? Well, I was good at reading people—maybe I could read trailers too. My gaze ran up and down them. I'd try the blue one near the middle.

I trudged back, hurrying this time, and ignoring the pain in my hands. I knocked on the trailer door before I could talk myself out of it.

No one answered.

I put the aquarium on my hip again, accidentally tilting it so Herman slid to one side. For a moment he looked like he was doing a snake version of the wave.

Maybe it was Steve Raleigh's trailer and he wasn't in. I tried the door and it opened.

So much for my ability to read trailers. I'd picked the makeup trailer. The lighted mirror had pictures of cast members taped to it. Makeup bottles and bobby pins cluttered the counter. I set the aquarium down with a defeated thud, then slid it under the counter. I couldn't carry it a second longer. I shook my hands to get blood flow back to them. After a few moments of that, I realized I couldn't pick the aquarium up again. I bent down to have a one-on-one with Herman.

"Look, just be a good snake for the day and then we'll take you back to the pet store, okay?" I took the lid off and tried to remember how the lady at the pet store had picked him up. Was it headfirst or by the middle? I reached in and lifted him out of the cage. He at once wrapped himself around my arm, which I hoped was not a sign he was trying to eat me.

I pushed the aquarium behind some boxes and headed out of the door, reminding myself that normal people didn't stop to chat with girls who walked around with large snakes. So Herman was my friend and I really shouldn't mind that he wanted to crawl up my arm. Which is what he was now doing. Maybe he was cold. After all, he'd been without a functioning heat lamp ever since the pet store. Most people who bought snakes probably took them home and plugged their lamps back in, as opposed to using the snakes to stalk celebrities.

Perhaps if I knocked on trailer doors, I could find someone who would tell me where Steve was. I headed to the next trailer, but before I'd reached it, the door flung open and Maid Marion—Esme Kingsley herself—strolled out. A woman wielding a can of hair spray followed after her. The woman did her best to spray Esme's long blond curls as she walked, but mostly managed to create an aerosol cloud.

I watched them, transfixed. I didn't even like Maid Marion, but seeing her pop into my sight tilted the world, made it all seem unreal.

Esme stopped short, and her hairdresser nearly bumped into her.

"This dress isn't right." Esme pulled at the waistline. "See how loose this is?" It wasn't very loose, but the woman nodded anyway. "I distinctly told them I wanted form-fitting. I'll look fat in this. Go get Angelique. Right now."

Esme gave me the impression of a vase full of cut roses. Beautiful. Elegant. But she was all for show and had absolutely no intention of ever growing again. And she had sharp thorns.

She turned on her heel and strode back into her trailer. The other woman headed to the studio building, still clutching the aerosol can. I'd been so wrapped up watching them, I only now noticed the security guard strolling across the grounds in my direction. Without another thought, I followed after the hair spray lady, jogging to catch up. "Hey, wait up!"

Herman didn't appreciate the bumpy ride. I felt his muscles flexing around my arm, and he slithered toward my shoulder.

Still, now that I walked side by side with Esme's personal hair-sprayer, I hoped the security guard would think I belonged here. I smiled over at her. "I'm going to need someone to get the door for me. As you can see, my hands are full."

She looked over at the snake disdainfully. "Is that real?"

Only on a Hollywood set would someone ask you if the snake crawling up your shoulder is real.

"He's harmless," I said.

She opened the door for me, then hurried past me, either because she wanted to fulfill Esme's wardrobe commands or because she wanted to put distance between herself and a five-foot python.

Since I was already inside the studio and a security guard was walking around by the trailers, I might as well look around inside for Robin Hood. I headed down the hallway. Did this place have a break room? I had no idea where I was going, but walked with purpose anyway.

Before long it felt like I had walked into the bowels of some strange fantasy land. I had to keep myself from staring at large painted backdrops of forests and mountains. I went past a room filled with mannequin heads. I'm sure the room had other things stored in it too, but once you see a crowd of disembodied faces staring back at you, you don't really notice anything else.

I kept walking, kept looking. A few people gave the snake curious glances, but no one said anything to me. A clock I passed read 11:45. I'd been here for almost an hour. I tried not to count how much time I had left until I had to leave. Off in the distance I heard voices and wondered if they were shooting something right now. What would happen if a girl in jeans and a baseball cap—not to mention wielding a large snake—wandered into the middle of a tender Robin Hood and Maid Marion scene?

I passed a man flipping through a stack of papers. He held his clipboard down when he saw me. "What's the snake for?"

I was in trouble. In the three seconds it had taken him to speak, I could sense his competency. The authority flowed off of him like heat waves on hot pavement. I wasn't going to be able to talk my way around him. I smiled and shrugged anyway. "They need it for the shoot."

"What shoot?" he asked. "We're only using horses today."

My insides grew brittle. "Oh. Maybe I looked at the wrong schedule then. I thought my boss told me it was snake day."

"Snake day? Which script calls for a snake?"

"Um, I really don't know. I was just doing what I was told."

"Who told you to bring in a snake?"

I said the only name which would make sense. "Mr. Powell."

At the director's name, the man backed off from me

a bit and looked thoughtful. To himself he said, "Why would Dean want a snake in a nunnery?" Then louder, he called, "Hey, Jim, can you come here for a sec?"

This would have been the appropriate time for me to see my life flash before my eyes, but my gaze stayed firmly on the man in front of me. My stomach, however, fell down to my knees.

When Jim didn't answer, the guy turned to me and said, "You stay here, and I'll find out what you're supposed to do."

Oh, I knew what I was supposed to do. I was supposed to go running down the hall wearing a snake who, during this conversation, had decided my neck was the most comfortable spot on my body. He was circling my collarbone like a reptile necklace.

"Okay," I said.

As soon as the guy turned away from me, I walked as quickly as I could back the way I had come. I couldn't run, as that would draw attention to myself; besides, if Herman grew frightened and tensed his muscles now, he might choke me. This is not how anyone wants the newspapers to report their death. *Girl choked by nervous python while fleeing movie set.*

I made it back down the hallway I'd come from, pushed open the door to the outside, and headed toward the trailers. Had my cover been completely blown, or did I have a few more minutes before security was called?

Before I could analyze this question, I noticed a security guy heading around the corner of the building. I wasn't sure if he was looking for me, but I wasn't about to take a chance. I ducked into the closest trailer. Which turned out to be the wardrobe trailer.

Clothes racks stretched across the room; rows of medieval dresses of every color surrounded me. Wimples, scarves, and headdresses hung on one wall. Shelves of shoes took up another wall. I couldn't see what was on the third wall because too many boxes were stacked up against it.

I ought to get away from the studio as fast as I could. I walked to the nearest box and opened it. It contained silk flower arrangements of pale pink roses. Well, not anymore. Now it contained silk flower arrangements and one large python. I shut the flaps of the lid, then looked for something to put over the box so Herman couldn't escape. Later I'd make an anonymous phone call from a pay phone somewhere in Burbank telling the receptionist to rescue him. I laid a pair of boots across the top of the box. He shouldn't be able to push that off, should he? How strong were Burmese pythons?

Instead of letting myself ponder snake skills, I took my cell phone and Jeremy's picture out of my pocket, then undressed and shoved my clothes into a corner. I took a long, velvety green dress from the rack and pulled it over my head. Security would be looking for a girl in a baseball cap, not a wandering extra. I'd be able to make it back to Madison and tell her we needed to leave. The dress didn't have pockets, so I put Jeremy's picture and the cell phone under my sash and tied it tight to keep them from falling out. I grabbed a circular cloth headband with a long cream train attached which fit over my head like a low-lying halo. I'd seen some other girls wearing them, so I would too.

I opened the door and peeked out to see if the coast was clear. The first thing I saw was the back of Robin Hood walking toward the studio building.

Chapter **7**

I recognized Robin Hood's feathered hat and tunic even from the back. He was already half the distance to the building ahead of me, but I hurried after him, hiking my long skirt up so I could run.

I crossed the distance to him, calling out, "Mr. Raleigh. Could I—"

He turned around and I stopped in my tracks. It wasn't Steve Raleigh at all. It was only a man dressed to look like him. My mouth hung open and I stared at him.

He smiled back at me. "Fooled you, didn't I?" When I didn't answer, he lifted his hands as though he'd told a joke I didn't get. "I'm the stunt double. I bet for a moment you thought: Wow, Steve Raleigh sure looks different in real life."

No, actually, I thought the last remnants of my sanity had suddenly dissolved, but I didn't tell him that. I only smiled weakly. "You just startled me." After I'd caught my breath, the incongruity hit me. "I thought Steve Raleigh did his own stunts."

"He does a lot of them. More than the studio suits would like him to, anyway. That's the thing about teenagers. They think they're immortal. Steve has a particularly bad case of believing his own press."

Leather medieval boots don't make a lot of sound on the ground, which is the only reason I didn't hear anyone approaching until a voice near my shoulder said, "What's not to believe?"

Then I jumped half a foot. When I turned, I stood face to face with Steve Raleigh. He looked like I'd seen him every night on TV, a blond-haired Robin Hood glowing with confidence and masculinity. His shoulders looked broader today. The tunic emphasized his muscular build, and his eyes had warmth that never accurately came across on TV.

I said, "Uh . . . uh . . . ," which luckily he paid very little attention to because the stunt double spoke again.

"You'll be glad to hear the horses all survived."

Steve sent him one of his trademark smirks. "Hey, if you're going to keep dropping out of trees onto them, you'd better cut back on the cheeseburgers. That's all I'm saying." Steve turned his attention to me, and the warmth stayed in his eyes. "You're new here?"

I nodded.

"Let me be the first to warn you. You can't believe anything this guy tells you."

The two men started toward the building again, and I walked between them, keeping my eyes trained on Steve. How could I bring up the subject of Jeremy? I'd messed up so badly yesterday; I needed to think of the perfect way to ask him to help me.

When we came to the studio door, Steve held it open for me. He watched me with questioning eyes as I walked past him. "You look familiar. Have I worked with you before?"

My heartbeat sped up. "No, I just started as an extra."

We continued down the hallway, but his eyebrows drew together. I knew he was trying to figure it out, and if he did, he would not be happy with me.

"My little brother idolizes you," I said. "He's six."

This seemed to momentarily stop him from examining my face. "Well, he's got taste for a six-year-old. I beat out Superman?"

"Oh, yeah. You beat out Santa Claus."

He glanced over at the stunt double with a smile. "And who says today's kids aren't well educated?"

We approached a doorway; even from several feet away, I could hear the noise of machinery and people's voices. In another minute our conversation would be over, but I couldn't bring myself to blurt out my request. It would be too easy to say no to it that way. I needed to let Steve know more about Jeremy. "He wants to be a Merry Man when he grows up," I said.

The stuntman tilted his head and chuckled. "Tell him to be a lawyer instead. They drive nicer cars."

I looked into Steve's eyes, trying to hold his attention with my gaze. "Last Halloween he dressed up as you." I wanted to take the picture out of my sash, but wasn't sure if Steve would understand if I suddenly started undressing in front of him. "He even carried his bow and arrows with him." I was about to add, "He has cancer." Only I never got that far.

An older woman stepped out of the doorway, and when she saw Steve, she motioned for him to come. "There you are. Dean wants to do some more close-ups before they run through the master shot."

"I thought he was working with Esme."

"And Esme is late. Again. So now she'll do hers after the master shot, and you're doing yours now."

Steve let out a disgruntled breath. "I swear, one of these days I'm just going to let King John kill her." He pushed ahead of me and walked through the door. I followed after him, but both he and the stunt man had lost any interest in talking to me. After a few more steps of watching two matching backs pull away from me, I stopped trying to catch up with them. To the air I said, "He's very sick."

No one heard me.

My gaze momentarily left Steve and took in the set. The room was huge. Seriously, if it hadn't been for all of the stuff inside, you could have had several NBA teams playing full-court basketball in here. Off to my left a knee-high miniature replica of a medieval village lay across the floor. I recognized it as one of the villages from the series. It had little cottages, thatched roofs, farms, and haystacks.

I didn't stare at it long. In front of me, and far more impressive, was a life-size reproduction of a medieval courtyard complete with a wall of ragged gray stones, large fishpond, and rustic benches. The bushes surrounding the pond looked real, as did the vines that grew up the wall of the building.

But the gardens beyond the fishpond were just a painted backdrop, and the tree trunks didn't belong to actual trees at all. The branches that hung down were attached to wooden scaffolding from the ceiling. The stone wall only went up about thirty feet and then stopped. There was no building, no other connecting walls or a roof.

It all felt surreal, as though this place were caught between two different worlds.

A man handed Steve a sword, gave him some last-minute instruction, and then left the set. Steve walked in front of the wall where a large camera on wheels scooted toward him.

Someone called, "Quiet on the set!" I looked toward the voice and recognized Dean Powell from the picture I'd seen on the internet. He sat in front of a video monitor, held a bullhorn to his mouth, and yelled, "Action!"

Steve swung his sword, fighting with the air in front of him. He did this for nearly a half an hour straight, lunging forward and backward with a self-assured expression. I stood there watching, waiting.

The hands of the clock had passed twelve-thirty and were creeping toward one. A security guard walked by, scanning the crowd. He spoke into his earpiece as he surveyed the room. "I don't see anyone matching that description, but I'll keep looking."

I went and stood by the other girls in medieval dresses to look less conspicuous.

After the cameraman finished filming close-ups of Steve sword fighting, they brought in another swordsman to film over-the-shoulder shots. It wasn't the actor who played Sir Guy of Gisborne, but a man dressed to look like him from behind.

Every minute of the fight had been choreographed. When the sword slipped out of Steve's hand during the first take, they repeated the performance step for step, swing for swing, during the second. The director had them redo it for a third time because he wanted Steve to look more determined.

One of the girls who stood near me watched him with hungry eyes. "I wonder if he ever gets tired."

The other said, "I never get tired of watching him."

Which is when I realized I'd been staring at him rather earnestly myself.

When the scene ended, one of the crew members brought Steve a bottled water. While he drank it, the director went over to talk to him. They spoke for a few moments, then walked in my general direction. I took a few steps to my left to make sure they'd have to walk by me, then I willed Mr. Powell to go away so I could have two minutes alone with Steve.

He didn't. Which perhaps didn't matter, since Steve didn't notice me at all. His attention did focus on something behind me, though. When I turned, I saw Esme strolling toward us, trailed by the hairdresser, who was still making adjustments to the curls in Esme's hair.

Although I seemed to be invisible to Steve, Esme's gaze came to a halt on my face. My first thought was that she recognized me—she'd seen me carrying the snake by her trailer and now she wondered why I was dressed in a medieval gown on the set.

Without a word in my direction, and while the hairdresser still shoved bobby pins into her hair, Esme turned to Mr. Powell with pursed lips. "I thought I made it clear that none of my ladies-in-waiting were to be pretty girls. The audience is supposed to look at me, not check out the extras behind me."

Both Steve and Mr. Powell turned and appraised me. I felt my cheeks growing bright red, and I fingered the fabric of my dress nervously.

Steve's gaze left me, and he sent an easy grin in Esme's direction. "Don't be ridiculous. No one is as pretty as you are. I've heard you say so yourself."

"Shut up," she told him, and turned to Mr. Powell with arched eyebrows.

He waved a hand in my direction. "Go change into one of the nun's costumes."

"How is that better?" Esme asked. "Do you want the audience to watch the fight or to wonder who the hot nun is?"

Steve looked up at the ceiling, then back at Esme. "I'll tell you a secret. Guys don't usually check out girls dressed as nuns. It would be creepy."

Esme put her hands on her hips, but Mr. Powell just shrugged. "The camera won't be close enough to see her features." He waved his hand in my direction again. "Go. You don't have much time before we start the master shot."

I went. As I left, I heard Esme still protesting that her contract guaranteed her certain things. I was so close, so close to speaking to Steve. And so close to being caught.

I walked back to the wardrobe trailer. I was going to be late heading back to Nevada, but how could I leave now? I'd think of some excuse and call my parents later.

This time a middle-aged woman stood among the costumes, taking several versions of the same Maid Marion dress out of dry-cleaning bags and hanging them up. She didn't question me about needing a nun's outfit, just produced one from the rack, held it up to me for size, and then handed me a matching wimple.

I changed while taking nervous glances at the box I'd put Herman in. I had put a pair of boots on top of that box, hadn't I? Maybe the wardrobe lady had seen them sitting there and put them away. I didn't see Herman crawling around anywhere, so maybe he'd curled up inside and taken a nap. At least I hoped so. All I needed was for the wardrobe lady to find a five-foot python in her trailer and call the security guards.

Thankfully, the nun's outfit had pockets. At least this way I'd be able to show Jeremy's picture to Steve without it looking like I was undressing to do it. And I needed to talk to Steve soon or it seemed likely I would be drafted into the master shot, whatever that was. I hoped it didn't require that I actually know anything about acting.

When I went back to the set, I saw Steve, but before I could walk in his direction, the director's assistant herded me over to a corner of the set where four other nuns stood waiting. Apparently, we were about to make some sort of nun procession. While the crew members adjusted the lights and fluffed up the foliage by the fishpond, the other nuns filled me in on what we were supposed to do. Which was the only benefit I could see from my recent demotion from lady-in-waiting to nun. I had a reason to be clueless.

We were about to do the OFS—obligatory fight scene—and in this particular episode, Maid Marion was stuck at a nunnery. Sir Guy had captured Robin Hood earlier in the show, imprisoned him in a dungeon, and had told Maid Marion that Robin would be executed if she didn't agree to be Sir Guy's bride.

When Sir Guy came onto the set demanding Maid Marion's answer, the mother superior and some of the nuns would try to keep him from seeing her, as we were not only holy sisters, but apparently also not big fans of Sir Guy.

His men would overpower us, then Sir Guy would yank Marion to her feet and say, "You have made a fool of me long enough. What is your answer?"

Robin Hood—who has, not surprisingly, escaped from the dungeon with the help of his Merry Men—was going to gallantly appear on yonder tree limb and say, "My answer is that you are a fool and will always be one."

Robin Hood would then use his bow and arrow to take out a couple of Sir Guy's men. Robin Hood, by the way, never shoots Sir Guy, even though Sir Guy is frequently standing right in front of him. This is one of the things that bothers me about the *Teen Robin Hood* show, but I was not about to bring that up. I just kept nodding as the other nuns filled me in on the story line.

Anyway, Robin Hood was going to swing down the tree from a rope—cynical viewers might wonder when he had time to set that up—and have a sword fight with Sir Guy. The result of which would be Sir Guy falling in the fishpond and Robin Hood yelling out, "You play the fool very well indeed!" before he rides off with Maid Marion.

Even though the whole sequence would only take a few minutes of TV time, the cast had been shooting it all day. Close-ups, three-quarter and over-the-shoulder shots. We were about to run through the scene from beginning to end.

"Ninety percent of anything we do will be left on the editing room floor," the mother superior told me. "But that doesn't mean Mr. Powell won't hang us by our wimples if we mess up."

She showed me our marks—where we were to stand when the scene began and where we would stagger to when Sir Guy's men shoved us out of the way. I nodded at her and tried to remember everything she told me, but other things kept distracting me. Like the security guards prowling the edges of the set and the horse the handlers brought in. I also noticed Steve Raleigh climb up a ladder to a platform and try out the rope.

"Remember," the mother superior told me, "don't *act* the part. *Be* the part."

Just as Mr. Powell told us to take our places, I felt my cell phone vibrating in my pocket. I didn't take it out to look and see who was calling, as I didn't think this was something a medieval nun would do. Instead I followed the other nuns out onto the set trying to look saintly. The director called out, "Atmosphere!" which was the extras' cue to start moving about, and then "Action!"

Sir Guy rode up on his horse and had words with the mother superior. She spoke her lines to him with an equal measure of fright and disgust.

Personally, I thought it was very considerate of him to ride his horse into the courtyard so Maid Marion and Robin Hood would have some way to head off into the sunset together, but I tried to look at his men reproachfully anyway.

I turned when the mother superior got knocked to

the ground. I reached out to help her up, but one of Sir Guy's men grabbed me by the arm.

That's when reflex took over. I twisted away from the man, trying to break his grasp. This must have caught him off guard because his feet didn't move, even though he kept a hold of my arm. He teetered, swore, then fell sprawled out on the floor in front of me.

I stared at him in surprise. "Oh, sorry," I whispered.

Mr. Powell stood up and yelled into the bullhorn, "Cut!"

Chapter 8

*T*he movement of bodies immediately halted, and everyone turned to face the director.

"You—the pretty nun!" he called. "What do you think you're doing!"

Every pair of eyes found me. I clenched my hands so tightly my fingernails dug into my palms. "Sorry. It was a reflex. You know, when someone attacks you, you just automatically—"

"No, you don't," he said in a clipped voice. "You are a nun. Nuns don't fight back. Make another mistake and you won't work on this set again." He sat back down and waved a hand in our direction. "Everybody take your positions—and what is wrong with that horse?"

Everyone turned their stares from me to the horse. The horse didn't seem nearly as humiliated by the attention as I had been—probably because horses have never been to junior high and don't realize that when everyone stares at you like that it means social death.

The handler walked onto the set cooing at the horse, who kept moving its weight from one leg to another and twitching its ears.

"Something might be wrong with the saddle," the handler called back. "I'll check it out."

Mr. Powell waved his hand in the horse's direction. "That should have been done before. At the rate we're going, they'll put *Jeopardy* reruns in our time slot. Where's our backup horse?"

The handler bent down to loosen the saddle straps and calmly called back, "We don't need another horse. Samson's a professional. He'll be fine."

"A professional?" Mr. Powell yelled. "I'll give you a ten-minute break and then Samson will be a professional circus horse." He said other things, but since they weren't yelled into the bullhorn, I didn't hear them. At the announcement of a break, dozens of murmured conversations started. Several of Sir Guy's henchmen sat down on the floor. A few people wandered off the set and picked up water bottles. A makeup artist walked over to Esme and brushed powder across her forehead while another rearranged the hair on her shoulders.

I unclenched my fists. Little red fingernail marks dotted my palms. The other nuns moved away from me, as though associating with me would make them look bad to the director.

Well, the Hollywood life was already looking less glittery. In the half an hour I'd been an actress, I'd been insulted by the leading lady, yelled at by the director, and shunned by a group of nuns.

"You can't take it personally."

I looked up at the sound of Steve's voice. I hadn't heard him walk over, but now he stood in front of me. "Directors are just like that. They surgically remove all people skills from them during film school." He leaned closer to me and lowered his voice. "Besides, Dean has obviously never been to Catholic school or he'd know that a lot of nuns can hold their own in a fight."

"Thanks," I said, because I knew he was trying to make me feel better. "I didn't mean to mess things up for everyone."

He shrugged, and I couldn't help but notice the way his tunic emphasized his muscled physique. "If it hadn't been you, he would have found some other reason to stop the scene. Just watch. He'll make us do it a dozen times. By the time we're through, there won't be any water left in the fish pond. Sir Guy's outfit will have soaked it all up."

Over Steve's shoulder I noticed Esme approaching, and I knew I didn't have time to waste on small talk. "Can I ask you a favor?"

His eyes immediately clouded, and I wondered how many times strangers had asked him for favors. Still, he tilted his head and his voice took on a teasing tone. "Well, you can always ask."

Esme reached his side, disapproval making her face look hard and cold. I knew she was about to take him away from me. I felt it happening already.

I reached out a hand toward Steve, nearly touching his sleeve. "Can I just have you alone for two minutes?"

His head tilted back, and he raised an eyebrow at me, which is when I realized I had not phrased the question right. With eyebrow still raised, he said, "Oh?"

Esme snorted in my direction. "Two minutes? Well, you must work fast."

"No, I—"

Steve took a step away from me. "I'm sure you've heard all sorts of stories about celebrities, but I'm really not like that."

Esme smirked at him and crossed her arms across her chest. "That's right. One woman is pretty much like the rest to him."

"Where do you come up with these things?" he asked her.

I said, "I want to talk to you about my brother. He has cancer."

Steve's attention returned to me, but he only looked mildly interested. None of the shock and sympathy most people showed me appeared on his face. "You want a donation? You'll have to talk to my assistant. He takes care of that sort of thing." Steve scanned the room. "He's—where is Ron?"

Esme looped her arm through Steve's and slowly pulled him away from me. "He's probably arranging a hostile takeover of some poor, hapless company. Isn't that what you pay him to do?"

I held up one hand. "I don't want your money, just your time."

Steve let out a short laugh. "You'll have better luck asking for money. I have more of that. Find Ron and talk to him." Then Steve let himself be propelled away.

I took a step to follow them, but Esme shot me a piercing look over her shoulder. "It's unprofessional to bother celebrities during a shoot. And it's absolutely unthinkable to ask for money."

I stared after them, at first numb, until the humiliation seeped in. Then I felt my cheeks flush with embarrassment. I had never been so singularly dismissed in my life. And this after I'd told them my brother had cancer. I wasn't a con man. I wasn't some sort of freeloader. I'd asked for two minutes of his time, and he hadn't been willing to give me that much. How did a person become so calloused to others' suffering?

Well, what had I expected from someone who sued his own family?

I turned away from the sight of him and walked across the set. I meant to leave. I meant to walk back to Madison and tell her we were going home.

The director yelled, "Places, people!"

I kept walking.

"Hey, pretty nun!" the director yelled at me. "Get with the other nuns!"

I stopped as though pulled back by a leash. As much as I wanted to leave, I would draw too much attention to myself if I walked off the set now. The security guards, who were still prowling around the edges of the court-yard, would certainly notice me then. I gritted my teeth and stomped over to the other nuns.

The director held up one hand in the air. "And don't look so angry," he yelled as though I were tormenting him. "You're a nun, for heaven's sake!"

I took several deep breaths and stared at the ground, trying to regain composure. When I looked up, I saw Steve a few feet away, climbing his ladder but watching me. "You still look angry," he said.

"I'm just an extra," I told him. "You don't need to concern yourself with me."

"Listen, I'm sorry about your brother."

"Yeah." I sent him a cold smile. "I'm going to tell Sir Guy where you're hiding as soon as he arrives."

Steve tilted his head back and laughed. Which only made me want to throw something at him.

"Atmosphere!" The director called. I knew I wasn't supposed to look at the camera, so I gazed across the set to where Esme and her ladies-in-waiting sat by the fishpond. It was the first time I noticed the pale pink roses that surrounded it. Roses like the ones I'd seen in that box. When had those flowers been brought in?

"Action!"

Sir Guy and his men came on. I gulped and didn't have to fake my worried expression. I did, however, find it hard to look at them when I really wanted to scan the set for a snake. My gaze kept darting around the scenery.

This time when Sir Guy's henchman grabbed me around the waist, I didn't fight back. I let out a pitiful-sounding "Ahhh!" then craned my head around to check for anything slithering around the floor behind me.

Sir Guy led the horse over to Maid Marion, let go of the reins, and pulled Marion to her feet. The horse shook its mane and took a step away from the roses, but the director either didn't notice or didn't care.

"You've made me a fool long enough," Sir Guy said. "What is your answer?"

Maid Marion blinked up at him, a tearful expression on her face.

Robin Hood stepped out on the tree limb. "My answer is that you are a fool and will always be one."

Robin Hood let two arrows fly in quick succession, although not the kind of arrows with tips that could actually hurt anyone. I supposed that was one of those parts they edited in later. Still, Steve managed to hit two of Guy's men, including the man who held on to me. The henchman gave an impressive-sounding groan and dropped to the ground.

The director must have been paying attention to the henchman's performance and not Steve's face, or he would have complained. Because Steve gazed at me— at first it was only a glance because I was in his line of vision—but then a questioning look flickered across his expression. He was trying to figure something out. After a moment, he seemed to remember he needed to go on with the scene and he took hold of the rope. He jumped, but midair his eyes swung back to find me.

Recognition filled his face, and I knew he had placed me.

Which is probably why, instead of dropping to the ground in front of Maid Marion, he actually plowed into her and sent her flying into the fishpond.

An impressive splash shot up, followed by an even more impressive scream. I could hardly hear the director call "Cut!" over it.

Sir Guy burst out laughing, which didn't help matters. As Maid Marion floundered around, trying to stand in a now waterlogged dress, he called out to her, "I've changed my mind. Robin can have you!"

Steve stepped into the pool to help Esme, but she stood up and pushed him away. "Do you think this is funny? There are fish in this pond! A carp ran into me! I probably have carp crap in my hair now."

I'm not sure whether it was the yelling or the splash that convinced Herman to make a run—or rather slither—for it, but he shot out of the bushes, sweeping across the floor making giant S's.

The horse noticed this new event right away. He whinnied, reared on his back feet, and proved he was indeed a professional. Or at least could have been a professional tap dancer, since this is what it looked like as he stomped the floor in an effort to keep Herman away.

Say what you will about snakes' intelligence, Herman was smart enough to make a beeline, or in this case an S-line away from the horse, and into the group of ladies-in-waiting. They all screamed and jumped up on top of the benches, except for one who ran into the fishpond, pushing Esme down again as she did.

More splashing. More screeching. All of this commotion spooked the horse further, and he galloped off the set, scattering nuns in his wake. The last I saw of him, several crew members and the handler were chasing him through the miniature thatched village.

The director yelled things at the top of his lungs, most of which weren't actually directions. However, in between a lot of cursing, he did tell us to "Clear the set!" and I intended to.

I turned to follow my fellow nuns. I'd even taken several steps in that direction when Steve grabbed my arm and spun me around.

"You're that girl from the basketball game, aren't you?" He gripped my arm harder, and his eyes grew cold. I couldn't breathe. I stared back at him with my mouth forming a response that didn't come.

Two security guards appeared behind him, peering down at me. They didn't say anything, just watched Steve speak with me.

"You're some sort of stalker, aren't you?" he said.

"No." I tried to take a step away from him but couldn't budge out of his grip. "See, a stalker would have known you had brown hair. I only wanted to talk to you."

"How did you get past security? How did you get a costume and a part on this series?"

I glanced at the security guards, who looked more menacing by the moment. "Is that a rhetorical question or do you actually want to know?"

"How about this—you can tell it to the police." Steve let go of my arm, which was apparently the signal for the security guards to flank me on both sides.

"You don't need to do that," I said.

One of the security guards took hold of my elbow. "We'll go ahead and contact the police for you, Mr. Raleigh."

I kept my eyes on Steve. "No. Please."

He stared at me, his expression unmoved, and didn't reply.

The other security guard nodded in Steve's direction. "We'll take her to the guard station until the police get here. You'll need to come by and make a statement for them then."

I shook my head, looking for something besides anger in Steve's face. I could barely speak. "Don't make them take me to the guard station."

The guard's grip tightened around my arm. For a second, Steve's gaze traveled from my face to the guard's hand. I could tell he'd decided something. "Take her to my trailer," Steve told the men. "I'll deal with her after I'm done here."

"To your trailer?" the first guard asked.

"Yeah. And make sure she doesn't leave."

The security guards looked at one another, and perhaps they would have said something else, but when they turned back, Steve had already left.

The security guards looked at each other again, and the first—a Pacific Islander who probably ripped trucks apart in his spare time—grunted in disbelief. The second shrugged and said, "So we take her to his trailer."

The first guard pulled me by the arm, and we walked off the set. I tried to decide if it was a good thing that I was going to Steve's trailer instead of the guard station. Probably not. Steve hadn't looked like he wanted to sit down and have a friendly chat. He most likely just wanted to find out how I'd managed to find him twice so he could avoid future stalkers, and then he'd turn me over to the police.

We went out of the building at a fast pace. I had no choice but to keep up. The guard never loosened his grip on my arm. The second security guard had gray streaks in his crew cut. He was probably at least forty, but his biceps were as big as my head, so he was still quite imposing. He didn't say anything at all, just kept nodding and grunting in approval as the first guard lectured me about trespassing, privacy, and how celebrities had the right to live normal lives without worrying about fans who didn't have the sense to know when not to cross the line.

"I've learned my lesson," I told them. "Really, you can let me leave now—"

But they didn't. Crew-cut guy led me to a large green trailer.

So Steve's was the green one. It figured. Robin Hood wore all green, and it hadn't even occurred to me his trailer might be the green one.

The Polynesian guard released his grip on my arm.

"How many people came with you when you decided to invade the set today?"

I was not about to turn Madison in. "Just me."

"You're lying." He said this with an assurance that surprised me. Usually people couldn't tell when I lied. "How many of your little friends do we have to round up—the truth this time."

I didn't answer him, even though he asked twice more.

This led the guards to have a minute-long conversation about how they needed to split up and continue searching the grounds. They decided the Polynesian guy would search through the trailers while the older guy stayed with me. He would stand guard outside the trailer so he could keep an eye out for other teenage encroachers and still make sure I didn't run off.

Crew-cut opened the door and pointed inside. "Wait in there. And don't touch anything. You don't want to get yourself in more trouble than you're already in."

I turned away from them and walked up the steps into the Winnebago. The door shut behind me with a determined thud.

I guess I expected the inside of a star's trailer to be glamorous. Maybe a hot tub, a fireplace, and a shelf full of Oscars. Instead it looked like a cramped apartment. The living room had built-in couches and a TV that pulled down from the ceiling. Behind it, cabinets lined a small kitchenette. A door stood behind the kitchen—probably leading into a bedroom and not outside. Mini blinds let light in through windows on either side of the walls. There was nothing glamorous about it.

The only really unusual thing about Steve Raleigh's trailer was that it wasn't empty. A middle-aged man sat on the couch directly in front of me.

Chapter 9

He looked nice enough, like a lot of people you'd walk by without giving much thought to. But he reminded me of a book: full of creativity inside. He stared down at his laptop, and I sensed him going through ideas like someone sorts madly through a laundry basket searching for a missing sock.

He looked up at me, deemed me unworthy of attention, and went back to typing.

"Um . . . who are you?" I asked.

His gaze stayed on the computer while his fingers clicked over the keys. "Jim Blasingame, one of the show writers. I'm waiting to talk to Steve about the next script. Who are you?"

"A nun who just got fired."

"Oh." He didn't stop typing. "What are you doing here?"

"Don't think I haven't asked myself that question." I

sat down on the couch in front of him but glanced over my shoulder. I could see the back of the security guard standing by the side of the door.

When I returned my attention to Mr. Blasingame, he had stopped typing long enough to consider me, but then he shook his head. "Oh, never mind, I don't really want to know. I need to finish this script. Will Steve be here soon?"

"Yes."

He waved a hand in my direction. "Good. Then do whatever it is fired nuns do, quietly."

The sound of his typing—and then almost obsessively pushing the delete button—filled the room.

I sat on the couch and pulled my knees up to my chin. I couldn't believe it was going to end this way. I had worried I wouldn't be able to speak to Steve Raleigh; I had even considered the possibility that he wouldn't help me, but I had never imagined myself trapped in his trailer waiting for the police to haul me away.

I wished I could cry. I might have even garnered some sympathy from the writer—or from Steve whenever he came back. I'm not sure where the body keeps its reservoir of tears, but as always mine wasn't there. It had been dammed up, frozen over, drained. I only had a huge empty space I occasionally wandered around in, kicking up dust.

I sat for a while longer listening to the tap of the keyboard while the feeling of doom penetrated down to my bones. I wanted to say a prayer, but I wouldn't. My last official prayer had been before Jeremy's first MRI. I'd said, God, if you love me at all, even a little, you'll make it so the MRI shows everything is normal. When it came back as a tumor, I couldn't pray anymore.

Part of me knew I was being childish. Bad things happen to people sometimes. And everyone dies sooner or later. But things like this shouldn't happen to six-year-olds. They just shouldn't. It felt like God had tossed my family aside, like he didn't care what happened to us.

I got up, walked into the kitchenette, and leaned against the counter. I needed to call Madison and tell her what had happened. As I turned sideways for privacy I noticed a compound bow leaning against the wall. A Conquest Four. It was bigger and newer than mine but basically the same type. A quiver full of arrows sat on the counter. Steve must use them to practice with.

I touched the bow, running my fingers down the cable. It reminded me of my story for Jeremy and that I still needed to figure a way to get the two of us out of the underworld. Braided hair hadn't worked—did they have rope lying around the underworld? How should we escape?

Before my mind could move on to the next thought,

a feeling of icy darkness swept around me. I struggled to breathe. It was as if the Grim Reaper himself stood directly behind me. I could feel him leaning over my shoulder, could hear his hollow, grating breath near my ear. "You can't escape," he said. "You'll never find a way."

I gasped and spun around. "Stop it!" I yelled. But there was nothing there.

For someone who'd always put a lot of stock in my sanity, this wasn't a pleasant experience. I put one hand across my eyes. "It's no wonder I can't sleep anymore."

That's when I noticed the typing had stopped. I looked over and saw Mr. Blasingame staring at me. I ran my hand through my hair. "I'm just working on some lines for an audition."

"Oh." He nodded and for the first time admiration crept into his voice. "You're really good."

"Thanks."

He went back to his computer, and I leaned against the counter, trying to slow my heart rate. It felt like my insides had crashed through a window. I wondered what would happen if Jeremy didn't recover from his cancer. Would I walk around forever with shards of glass cutting into my thoughts?

I pulled my phone from my pocket with still trembling hands. It had a message from Madison. I'd missed her call during my brief but eventful stint as an actress. I listened to it, mostly because I wanted to put off telling her I'd been caught.

On the message she said, "So do we look alike? Apparently the security people here think we do because when they came looking for a girl who'd sneaked onto the lot wearing a baseball cap and carrying a snake, they singled me out." Which, I suddenly realized, was the reason the security guard knew I was lying when I told them I'd come here alone. They'd already caught Madison.

I could hear her disgruntled sigh on her message. "And don't you dare tell me it was my fault for not looking like I belonged. I sat there with the rest of crew eating doughnuts. In fact I'm pretty sure I gained five pounds fitting in. But they caught me." She sounded ashamed to admit this, and I wasn't sure whether it was because she hadn't been stealthy enough to avoid detection or whether the humiliation of being caught doing something wrong was just too much for her. Probably the latter.

"The security guards kept asking me what I'd done with the snake," she continued. "I told them I had no idea what they were talking about. Which became a lot less believable when they escorted me to your van and saw the cages of rabbits and doves.

"Anyway, they made me leave and said they'd call

the police if I came back. So I just returned the doves and bunnies to the pet store." There was a pause, and I wondered if she'd ended her message but then she added, "I hope you're having better luck. Give me a call when you can."

I guess it had been too much to hope that she was somewhere near, or that she would have a great idea for rescuing me. When I called her, I knew she would insist on calling our parents.

But it was better if I broke the news to them. My cell phone clock read 1:52. I fingered the buttons on the phone and wondered who I should call. Would Mom be more upset or would Dad? And what was I going to say?

Dad, I have some good news and some bad news. The good news is, depending on how things are edited, I may appear in an upcoming episode of Teen Robin Hood.

The bad news is you have to come get me out of a jail in Burbank.

Or: *So, Mom, you know how you've always encouraged me to follow my dreams? Did it ever occur to you that some of those dreams might get me arrested?*

No matter who got me, I'd have to face both of them knowing how horribly I'd failed.

I looked at my cell phone, but I couldn't call. I sat there leaning against the counter and watched the minutes appear and disappear on the face of the phone until it went dark again. I really only wanted to talk to one person, Jeremy.

I debated this for a few moments. He was in school. I shouldn't interrupt his class with a phone call, I shouldn't bother him. But, then again, it was first grade—so what if he missed a few minutes of cutting or pasting? I wanted to hear his voice. Besides, I had to tell him I wouldn't be home after school again.

I called the school, and they put me through to his classroom. The teacher told me the class was at music right now. I told her Mrs. Palson was picking Jeremy up after school and I needed to talk to him about the change in plans. I must have sounded desperate enough, because she told me she'd go get Jeremy.

A few minutes later, his voice came on, sounding older than he really was.

"Hey, Buddy," I forced some cheer into my voice. "I'm going to be busy after school, so you're going to Gabe's house again, okay?"

"Okay," he said.

He sounded like he was about to hang up, so I quickly added, "I didn't get to see you last night. What did you guys do?"

"Mom and me started planning my birthday party," he said. "Do you think they have birthday parties in heaven?"

"Um. . . ." Those kind of questions always caught me off guard.

"Dad says they do, but Mom started crying and wouldn't answer me."

"Well, they probably do, but I thought you wanted to have your next party at Chuck E. Cheese's. Remember, you're supposed to think positively. Envision seven candles on your birthday cake and a giant singing rodent standing behind you."

I must have said this last part too loudly because Mr. Blasingame looked at me peculiarly. I turned away from him and lowered my voice so he couldn't hear me anymore. "I, um, I'm probably not going to get home until late tonight, maybe not until after you're already in bed—"

"Then when are you going to finish the story about you and me and the Grim Reaper?"

"I'm not sure I want to finish that one."

"But you have to. We're both stuck in the under-world."

I knew he was right. I couldn't end the story without getting Jeremy out.

I looked over my shoulder, as though this would prevent the Grim Reaper from popping up again. "Where did I leave off?" I knew very well where I'd left off, but I stalled in order to give myself time to think.

"We were trapped in the underworld," Jeremy said. "But the dog liked me."

"Right. Everyone liked Jeremy because so many grandparents live in the underworld, and you know how they feel about little kids."

"What happened after the arrow wouldn't work?"

"Annie felt so sad her heart shattered into a thousand pieces, and when she cried the little pieces flowed out of her tears and into the palms of her hands. They didn't wash away, but instead crystallized into diamond dust.

"Birds always search for shiny things, and one little crow saw the sparkle of diamonds and flew back to the world and told all of his friends. Soon a giant flock flew toward them. When Annie saw them coming, she blew the dust on Jeremy until he sparkled—so of course the crows wanted to take him back to their home in the woods."

I heard the noise of voices in the background. The rest of his class must have come back in.

"But how could the crows leave the underworld?" Jeremy asked. "I thought that once something came it had to stay, even the animals."

"Animals are different," I said.

"Nuh-uh," he said. "Animals die; I see them squashed in the street all the time."

I heard the teacher's voice telling the kids to settle

down and take their seats. I didn't have long to finish my story. "Have you ever seen a dead crow in the street?"

He paused for a moment, thinking. "No."

"See? Crows are different."

"But crows aren't strong enough to carry a person." He said this with worry, and I wondered if I was about to instill a lifelong phobia of crows into him.

"Well, not the normal crows from our world."

"But you just said they were from our world."

Crows, it seemed, were not going to work as an escape route from the underworld.

I heard the teacher standing very close to Jeremy. "Are you ready to join the class?"

"I'll finish the story later," I told him. "You've got to go."

"I love you, Annika," he said, because per Mom's instructions we never say good-bye anymore.

"I love you too," I said, but I think he'd already hung up.

Next I called my mom. There was no point putting it off any longer.

She picked up the phone on the first ring. "Are you already out of school?" Before I could answer she said, "I had a client fall through, so I'm at the grocery store. I'm picking up some frozen enchiladas for you to eat while we're at the hospital with Jeremy. I thought you might enjoy a change since we've eaten organic for so long."

"That's great, Mom. Thanks." I nearly added, "It's probably better than the food they'll serve me in prison." But I didn't.

"If you'd rather I cook you something without preservatives, though, I can do that. I can make something up and freeze it for you."

"You don't have to."

She let out a gasp, and I heard the box rustle in her hands. "This says it has mono- and diglycerides. Those don't sound healthy. You don't want to eat this."

"Yes, I do."

There was a thunk like a box being thrown back into the freezer section, and her words came out choked with emotion. "No, I should be just as concerned with your health as I am with Jeremy's. I'll make you something nutritious."

"Mom. It will be all right. You can't catch cancer from eating enchiladas."

She paused for too long. "I know. I just worry. I'll find something else."

I wanted to tell my mother everything. I wanted to curl up in her lap, the way I did when I was little, and let her fix everything. But I couldn't. Not when she was nearly crying over enchiladas. She needed me to be the strong one now, the one that solved problems instead of creating new ones.

My feet weren't on solid ground, but I would tread water as long as I could to keep her from noticing.

"School hasn't ended yet," I said. "I was calling to tell you our chemistry teacher gave us a one-day extension on our project—which we really need. If I'm not home when you get home, it means that Jeremy is at Gabe's and I'm with Madison."

She let out an unhappy sigh. "You ought to be spending time with your family. We need to be together right now—"

"I know. I'll be home as soon as I can. I promise."

She sighed again, but in the end agreed. We said our non-good-byes, then I hung up the phone and glanced around the trailer. I had to escape and make my way back to Madison. I just wasn't sure how.

I took a few steps toward the living room. I could still see the back of the security guard out the front window of the trailer. A couple of times he'd glanced over his shoulder into the trailer to check on me, but right now he faced forward. Mr. Blasingame still sat on the couch, absorbed in his typing.

I stepped over to the window in the kitchen. It was completely sealed, with no way to open it. I walked to the window in the living room opposite the side where the guard stood. It had levers on either side and the words EMERGENCY EXIT printed on the bottom of the window frame. I could get out of this window if I could do it in a way that didn't draw attention from the guard or Mr. Blasingame.

My mind raced, trying to formulate a plan. How long would it take the crew to reset the scene and go through it again? The clock on the microwave read 2:15. Maid Marion had to change out of her wet clothes and blow-dry her hair. I might have long enough.

I opened the door in the back of the room. A bedroom complete with dresser and closet stood in front of me. "I'm going to change out of this nun's outfit," I called to Mr. Blasingame. "So don't come back here or let anyone else come back here, okay?"

"Okay." He put one leg over his knee, and I noticed he wore two different socks, both tan, but different shades of tan. Clearly, he wasn't the most observant man. I could use that to my advantage.

I shut the bedroom door, then called Madison while I riffled through Steve's dresser. I had to find some clothes I could fit into.

"Hey, Madison."

"Thank goodness you phoned. We need to leave for Nevada. Where are you?"

I found a light blue T-shirt and threw it on the bed. "I'm being held captive in Steve Raleigh's trailer."

"No, seriously, where are you?"

"I am serious. Steve recognized me in the middle of a scene, was overcome with surprise—or maybe karma—and ended up pushing Maid Marion into a fishpond. Then the snake got loose and frightened the horse, and there was a lot of screaming—mostly by the director but also some by the cast members—and so Steve told these security guards to put me in his trailer, and that's where I am. I think he's going to call the police after he's finished reshooting the scene."

"The police?" Madison's voice came out in nearly a whisper. "Have you called your parents?"

Steve had jeans in his drawers, but I knew none of them would fit me. After all, he was over six feet tall. Maybe I could find some sweatpants.

"I'm going to switch clothes, climb out of the window, and take one of the horses. Then I'll ride to town and find you."

There was a long pause. "Are you crazy?"

I took off my wimple and flung it on the bed. "Don't ask me that question. You might not like the answer."

Madison let out an aggravated breath. "Annika, you couldn't navigate your way through Burbank with Map-Quest and a van. You'd never make it on a horse."

I flung open one of Steve's drawers with too much force, and it nearly came all the way out of the dresser. "It's better than staying here and waiting for the police to pick me up. What have I got to lose?"

"Movement in a lot of your body if the horse throws you. Just start walking toward Burbank, and I'll pick you up with the van."

I opened the last drawer. I had to find something. I pulled out a pair of Bermuda shorts. They would have to do. "I'll call when I get past the front guard. Don't park anywhere too close to the studio. You can't let them see you."

I hung up the phone, unzipped my nun's outfit, and stepped out of it. Then I slipped on the T-shirt and pulled Steve's shorts on. They slid off my hips. I looked around for something to use as a belt. In his closet, I found an assortment of shoes. I took the laces out of one of them, wound it through two of the belt loops, and pulled them tightly together. Lastly I put my cell phone and Jeremy's picture into the pocket in Steve's shorts. I didn't bother checking the window in Steve's bedroom to see if it opened. Even if it did, it would lead to the front where the security guard stood.

Holding the nun's uniform, I stepped back into the living room. How was I going to get rid of Mr. Blasingame so I could get out of the window?

I walked over and stood in front of him. "Um, I'd like to go over some more lines. If it's too noisy for you in here, though, you can go back to the bedroom to work. It's really quiet back there."

"Here's the thing," he said as though we'd been in

the middle of a completely different conversation. "I don't know what to do with Maid Marion. It's always the same story. She gets captured, and Robin rescues her. I just can't write that one more time."

"Oh." I looked at the costume in my hands and then the throw pillows on the couch. The security guard hadn't turned around to check on me for some time, but I couldn't count on him to keep ignoring me. While I talked, I stuffed the wimple onto a pillow. "Well, could you write something completely different, like, say, fling Maid Marion into a fishpond?"

"What good would that do?" Mr. Blasingame looked up from his computer, but didn't seem to think it odd that I was turning a pillow into a proxy nun.

I shrugged. "It would give me, as a viewer, a lot of satisfaction to see her sitting in the middle of a fishpond."

The corners of Mr. Blasingame's lips tilted up, and he leaned back into his couch. "It might give me some satisfaction too, but I doubt I could stretch that out to a forty-four-minute plot line."

"Could you kill her off?"

"She's got a contract, but . . ." He leaned forward, typing again. "Maybe we think she's died but really she's got amnesia—" Almost immediately he put his finger on the delete button. "No. They couldn't cure amnesia in the Middle Ages. I'd write myself into a corner. What else have you got?"

I stuck the pillow between the back of the couch and the top cushion so it looked like my head was resting on the couch. "You could make her go insane. Maybe she could feel like Death was talking to her."

"No, too creepy. She'd lose all audience appeal."

I ignored the implications of that comment and laid my habit on the couch. From outside the trailer it would hopefully look like I was sitting there.

Mr. Blasingame typed for another minute, then stopped. "There needs to be something else. Something bigger."

I walked over to the emergency exit window, pulled the blinds all the way up, and looked out as though checking the weather. "She could die, end up in the underworld, and Robin Hood has to save her. *He* could probably figure out a way to do it."

Mr. Blasingame looked up from his keyboard so intently, I was positive he would ask me what I was doing. Instead he said, "That's already been done before."

"When?"

"*Hercules*. Disney. Every kid in the viewing audience has seen that movie. Shakespeare I could steal from, but not Disney."

"Hercules had an advantage the rest of us don't," I said and couldn't keep the bitterness from my voice. "He was immortal. My brother and I are stuck down there with nothing but a flock of crows to help us."

Mr. Blasingame didn't answer, just went back to his typing with a thoughtful look. It struck me that even my bizarre statement didn't faze him. Perhaps I wasn't going crazy after all. Perhaps I was just becoming a writer.

The clock read 2:28. I couldn't waste more time on trying to get Mr. Blasingame to move.

I undid the latch to the window on one side and then the next. I eased the pane sideways so it wouldn't crash to the ground. I had been prepared with an explanation of why I dressed the pillows in my nun costume— I needed someone to read my lines to—and I could perhaps say I'd taken the window out because I wanted fresh air, but I had no reasonable justification for crawling out of the trailer. I had to hope he didn't notice. Once I had the window out, I gently lowered it onto the trailer floor. Against the carpet, it didn't make a sound.

I took one last look at Mr. Blasingame to make sure he was still engrossed in his work, then as quietly as I could, I heaved myself out of the window. I landed on the ground with a thump. I didn't wait to see if he noticed my departure and was about to look out the window to see what I was doing.

The trailers were lined up next to each other, not touching but close enough to make a good screen from everything on the front side. Now I just had to stay behind them until I could make a run for it. I hurried toward the front end of Steve's trailer, trying to be as quiet as possible. I listened for the voice of the security guard.

I didn't hear it, but I did hear shouting come from inside of the trailer. Steve's voice. He'd come back.

Chapter 10

I peered around the edge of the Winnebago. The space between the trailers was clear right now, but I could hear footsteps thundering out of Steve's door and his voice shouting, "She can't be far. Drop to the ground and look for her feet."

Which meant in a moment they would see how very close I was. I did the only thing I could think of. I ran to the next trailer's back end, jumped on the fender, and shimmied up the ladder. Once I had reached the top of the trailer, I lay on my stomach, hoping no one would think to look up.

The warmth of the sun-baked roof pressed into my arms, legs, and face, along with tiny pieces of debris that bit into my skin. I lay there, willing myself to be one with the Winnebago.

I didn't dare lift my head to look, but voices rang out

below me. Crew-cut said, "I don't see anything. How long ago did Jim say she'd left?"

"A couple minutes," Steve said. "She couldn't have just disappeared."

"I'll call the other guards. We'll fan out and find her." A set of footsteps jogged away.

I listened for the sound of Steve's voice or his footsteps. I didn't hear anything, perhaps because the sound of my breath, coming in frantic spurts, was so loud.

Then I heard footsteps on the roof. I looked up and saw Steve, still dressed as Robin Hood, standing on the top of his trailer. He walked slowly over to the gap separating us. I got to my hands and knees, unsure which direction to go or what to do. I felt like a sprinter waiting for the gun to go off, only I didn't know which way to run.

He put his hands on his hips. "I thought you said you wanted to talk to me for two minutes."

"And I thought you said you were turning me over to the police."

"I still might. How did you get past the front guard and onto the set?"

I got to my feet and wiped the debris off my hands. "Look, I can't go to jail right now. I won't tell you anything unless you promise not to call the police."

He regarded me without worry. "You're stuck on the top of a trailer. I don't think you're in a position to bargain."

I took a step away from him, then another. "In the time it takes you to go back to your ladder, climb down, walk over here, and climb up this ladder, I'll be gone."

He tilted his chin down. "The trailers aren't that far apart. What makes you think I won't jump over?"

"Because you're the kind of guy who needs a stunt double."

He sent me an arrogant smile, then backed up in order to give himself a running start. I already stood a ways back from my edge, which gave me a second to weigh my options. Could I make the jump? He had the advantage of being taller and stronger.

He ran toward my trailer, I ran toward his. We both leapt. What I lacked in ability I made up for in determination. We passed each other in the air, then landed with two loud thunks.

He turned around and stared at me. "I can't believe you did that."

"You didn't leave me a lot of choices, did you?"

His lips pressed together in resolve. It wasn't just the costume—a Robin Hood glint passed through his eyes. I knew he didn't like being bested by a fraudulent extra. He took another run toward my trailer. I ran toward his. But it was one of those moments when being able to read people pays off. I knew he wouldn't complete the jump. He planned on stopping at the edge and watching me leap to his trailer.

I stopped at my edge too. The two of us stared at each other, only feet away.

He smiled at me, surprise and respect mingling in his expression. Then he backed up. "You know the problem with playing Rock, Paper, Scissors?"

I backed up too, matching his rate. "What?"

"Eventually you guess wrong."

He ran toward my trailer. I ran toward his. This time, I knew, we were both going over. He made jumping trailers look easy, but it wasn't. I pumped my arms hard and pushed my legs to go faster. The pounding noise of our feet momentarily paused as we glided past each other in the air.

I landed on the trailer and breathlessly turned to face him. "Actually, I never lose Rock, Paper, Scissors."

He took a few deep breaths, and his gaze ran up and down me, taking me completely in for the first time. "Hey—you're wearing my clothes."

"Yeah, sorry about that. The nun's outfit was a bit conspicuous."

With aggravation in his voice he said, "You can't steal that. That's my lucky poker shirt."

I glanced down at it. "Well, I don't think it's working. I'm not having a lot of luck so far."

He shook his head and laughed. I'd seen him do this on every episode of *Teen Robin Hood*, but it still mesmerized me. I couldn't do anything but stare back at him.

I heard footsteps from down below and looked to see Crew-cut hurrying toward the trailer. "There she is!" he yelled.

"Yeah, I noticed," Steve called back, "but don't climb up. She's half cat and doesn't realize she hasn't got nine lives."

The security guard stopped below me and, still panting, spoke into his earpiece.

"You don't have a choice anymore," Steve said calmly. "You'll have to come down."

"Are you going to turn me over to the police?"

"Maybe. Why so much concern? Do you already have a record?"

"No. I have a brother with cancer who's going into surgery on Friday morning." The words came out in a rush, and my voice broke. "I can't make my parents drive four hours to come bail me out of jail."

Steve's features momentarily softened, and he looked at me closer. "How old are you?"

"Seventeen."

He swore under his breath, and his eyes flashed with an emotion I couldn't place. "Climb down and meet me in my trailer. I won't turn you over to the police."

When I got to the front of Steve's trailer, both he and Crew-cut were waiting for me. The Polynesian guard walked quickly across the lot toward us. Perhaps they thought I'd run for it.

Steve held out one hand, making a sweeping motion toward the trailer door. "Ladies first."

I walked up the stairs without speaking to him, went inside, and sat sullenly on the couch. If he wasn't going to turn me over to the police, I didn't know why he didn't let me go and be done with it. I was probably in for a huge lecture, and frankly I didn't want to hear which laws I'd violated or how horrible I was to come here when I'd just been trying to help my brother.

If Steve had been straightforward with me at the basketball game, all of this could have been avoided. I would have learned last night that he didn't have a drop of compassionate blood in his body, and I could have been on my way home by now. Home to face failure.

Steve and the security guards walked into the trailer. Mr. Blasingame stood by the window, leaning out of it and peering up at the sky. "What was all that noise on the roof?"

Steve took off his hat and threw it onto a couch. "That was the sound of my teenage fan club and me leaping from trailer to trailer."

"I'm not your fan," I said.

"That's not what you said last night."

"And as I remember, you saw through that pretty quickly."

Mr. Blasingame pointed a finger at Steve in accusation. "You leapt across the trailers? Dean would kill you if he knew. The insurance people would kill you. Do you realize we're only halfway through shooting the season? Are you trying to give me a heart attack?"

Steve turned to me. "*That*, by the way, is why I have a stunt double."

Mr. Blasingame looked at me and waved a hand in my direction. "And what is going on with this girl, anyway? Since when did you start using your trailer as a brig, and when did I become a jailer?"

"I never said you were supposed to be a jailer." Steve crossed his arms and gave me a sharp look. "I only said a normal person would have questioned why someone would create a decoy nun and then crawl out the window."

Mr. Blasingame picked up his laptop from the couch and tucked it under his elbow. "Well, I'm not a normal person; I'm a writer." He walked over to me, shook my hand, and nodded approvingly. "You know, you've given me the perfect idea for next episode. Maid Marion escapes on her own and runs away—only she doesn't realize it's Robin Hood she's running away from. It's going to be gold."

With that, he walked out of the trailer whistling. We all watched him go. "He's right," the Polynesian guard said. "He's not normal."

Steve sat down on the couch in front of me. The

guards stood on either side of the door, like they were still on duty, which I suppose they were.

"Okay," Steve said, leaning forward. "First off, who are you?"

"You promise you won't turn me over to the police?"

"I promise."

I relaxed a little into the couch cushions. "My name is Annika Truman."

"All right then, Annika Truman. How did you get on the set today?"

My name sounded strange coming from his mouth. He wasn't on television acting this out. He sat in front of me, staring at me with eyes that could strike a girl mute. I brushed the sensation aside and told him the whole story. From the part where I'd promised Jeremy I could give him two wishes, to the point where I put the snake in the prop box.

Steve shook his head slowly. "You brought a snake into a place with horses?"

"I wouldn't have done that if I'd known they were using those flowers for your scene. I'm really sorry about all the screaming, and the people colliding in the fish-pond, and the horse trampling your little village—"

From behind me I heard the Polynesian guard chuckle. Steve glared at him.

"Did they find the snake?" I asked. "His aquarium is in the makeup trailer."

Crew cut said, "Yeah, one of the stagehands has him. I'll let them know." He took out a walkie talkie and said something into it.

"Look, Annika," Steve said, and the sound of my name on his lips distracted me for several more moments. "I'm really sorry about your brother—"

"Jeremy, his name is Jeremy."

"I'm really sorry about Jeremy—"

"Do you want to see a picture of him?" Before he could answer, I took the photo from my pocket. Steve's expression grew reluctant; he was already refusing me with his eyes. So I took the picture to the security guards first. They had no qualms about looking at Jeremy's photo.

"That was Jeremy at Halloween," I said. "He insisted on being Robin Hood. We had to search all over the place to find him boots that looked enough like the ones on the show."

Crew-cut took the picture. "He's a fine-looking kid." He nodded approvingly and passed the picture to the other guard.

The Polynesian guard pulled his wallet from his pocket. "Let me donate some money for him."

I took the photo from his hands. "That's okay. I didn't come here to ask for money."

Crew-cut had his wallet out too. He pressed a twenty-dollar bill in my hand. "I'm sure the medical bills are adding up."

Steve walked across the trailer to join us. "I already offered her money. I'm not completely heartless, you know." He took the picture from my hand. "Why are sick kids always so cute? Why couldn't just once, one of them look like a little troll who I wouldn't feel guilty saying no to?"

I took a step closer to Steve, one hand across my chest, pleading. "Please come see him. It would mean so much to Jeremy. I promised him his wish would come true. I *made* him believe. If he believes his wish came true, he'll believe he can make it through the surgery."

He handed the photo back to me and shook his head. "I would if I could, but the rest of my week is already booked. I'm supposed to meet someone at five tonight. I've got to work tomorrow, I have an awards ceremony tomorrow night I'm presenting at, and somewhere in the week I've got to go over the next script."

"Henderson is only four hours away—probably three and a half if you drive as fast as I do. If we left now and drove straight through, you could make it back in time—"

"To be exhausted to the point where I'm incoherent for tomorrow's shoot."

"You can sleep while I drive," I offered, but I could tell from his expression he wasn't even considering the possibility of coming with me. My throat felt tight, and it was suddenly hard to talk, but I did. I voiced my darkest worry, the one I'd pushed away every other time it had surfaced. I brought it out in the open, raw and painful, to show Steve.

"Jeremy might not make it through surgery; he's six years old, and he might be gone forever after Friday morning. The thing he wanted most in the whole world was for you to come and visit him. I'm sorry I barged in your life this way, but I thought if I could talk to you, if you understood. . . ." I kept my gaze on his, searching for a sign that he might relent. "I need you to grant him just one wish."

He shut his eyes, almost as if to shut out my gaze.

"I don't know how much time I have left with Jeremy," I went on. "And I gave up my time with him yesterday to drive here and talk to you. Couldn't you take a half a day out of your schedule to see him?"

Our eyes connected, and for a moment he didn't say anything. I didn't breathe, as though this would somehow help my case. Then he looked away from me. "I can give your brother a call before surgery. I can sign a picture. I'll even give him one of my arrows, but I don't have the time to go see him."

I had thought for sure I could persuade him to come with me. Even the security guards, who had started out acting as though they could cheerfully snap my limbs off, had been moved. But not Steve Raleigh.

I felt sharp pricks of disappointment needling my

heart. They would have turned into tears for most people, but in me they turned into stabs of anger. Still, I kept my voice even. "The real Robin Hood would have come with me."

Steve crossed his arms. "Yeah, well maybe that's because the real Robin Hood didn't have to spend all his time promoting his show. He also didn't have to meet with fencing, sparring, and archery instructors, and he didn't have to work out at the gym for two hours a day in case someone wanted to shoot a scene without his shirt on."

I knew it wouldn't do any good to make Steve mad at me when he could still charge me with trespassing, but at that point I just wanted to hurt him. "You're nothing like Robin Hood. In fact, if you lived in the Middle Ages you'd be the type who hangs around at King John's court so everyone would know how famous and important you are. You don't care about helping people at all."

He let out a slow breath, and his eyes grew hard. "You don't know anything about me." He swept his hand around the trailer as proof of what he said. "I spend more time being Robin Hood than Robin Hood did, and I bet I could outshoot him too."

"I bet you couldn't even outshoot me."

"Yeah, well, you'd lose that bet."

I took a step toward him. "Are you willing to wager on that? We'll have a shooting match. If I win, you're mine for the next"—I decided to add a cushion of time—"eleven hours. If you win, I'll never bother you again, and I'll promise not to call the tabloids and tell them how awful you are."

"How awful I am—because I won't drop everything and drive to Nevada with a stranger? You think the tabloids would buy that story?"

I shrugged and smiled. "I'm a pretty teenage girl with a sick little brother. A whole room full of people saw you order the security guards to hold me captive in your trailer."

Steve's gaze ran over me, sizing me up. "What are you, some sort of teenage mercenary?"

"I can cry on demand in front of news cameras," I lied, and held out my hand to shake his. "Do we have a wager?"

He looked up at the ceiling and then back at me, his frustration evident. "And when I win you promise you won't beg, stalk, or attempt to blackmail me anymore?"

"Right."

He shook my hand.

And it was foolish, I know, but I couldn't help the tingling sensation that I felt where he touched me. I thought: Steve Raleigh is holding my hand.

Chapter 11

We set up the target behind the trailers, then Steve and I stood about sixty feet away. Steve nocked an arrow and drew the bowstring without looking at me. The muscles in his arms flexed, and his eyes narrowed in on the target, examining it. He held the arrow in position for a moment, then let it fly. I knew it was a good shot even before it hit the target, just inside the bull's-eye.

It would be hard to beat him but not impossible.

He handed me the bow and an arrow. "I'm sorry, Annika."

"Don't apologize until you know what you're sorry for." I nocked the arrow onto the string. Steve's bow was bigger than mine, and I hoped that wouldn't throw me off. I held the bow steady and judged the distance. I'd made thousands of shots, made more bull's-eyes than I could count, but none ever mattered as much as this one. I could hit the mark if the nervousness didn't make my hand shake.

This is for Jeremy, I told myself. It has to be good.

I released the arrow, willing it to fly straight. It was almost a prayer, but not quite.

The arrow sang as it flew through the air. It hit, dead center in the bull's-eye.

I smiled and handed Steve back his bow. "Now you know what you're sorry for. You're sorry you have to drive to Nevada with a stranger."

He stared at the target openmouthed and then turned to me. "How did you do that?"

"I'm president of my high school archery club." I shrugged and gave him a smirk of my own. "Well, you didn't think I watched your show because of the sophisticated drama, did you?"

The guards walked up, simultaneously shaking their heads. "That was some fine shooting," Crew-cut said.

"Thanks." I smiled over at Steve. "And I've changed my mind about your shirt. It might be lucky after all."

Steve waved a hand in my direction. "She's president of her high school archery club! She never got around to mentioning that fact."

"Must be a good club if she can beat you," Crew-cut said. "How many hours do you practice a week?"

Steve crossed his arms and gave the guard a dark look. "I don't want to talk about it."

I shrugged again. "If it's any consolation, I'm sure you could beat me at fencing."

His dark look turned on me. "You want a rematch, then?"

"No. We made a bet, and I won. Do you want to take your car or my minivan? Although I probably should warn you there may be doves and rabbits inside. I'm not sure whether Madison's managed to get rid of those or not."

Steve ran his fingers through his hair, then held his hands out to me as though showing me something. "I can't go. I've got things I need to do here. I've got scenes to shoot tomorrow, and the awards ceremony is a very big deal. A producer I need to talk to will be there—"

"You promised." I put my hands on my hips. "Do you keep your word or not?"

"I can't just leave with you. I don't know anything about you. Do your parents even know you're here doing this?"

I sent him a slow grin. "I guess those are things you should have thought about before you promised to come with me."

Steve looked heavenward for a moment, then back at me. "Fine. You have me for eleven hours and only eleven hours. Less, if it doesn't take that long. I will talk to your little brother, and I will leave. I won't chat with your friends, pose for pictures, or give an exclusive to your hometown newspaper. I'm there and I'm gone. Understood?" He walked back to his trailer, gripping the bow. I followed after him, pulling out my cell phone to check the time. It was a little after three-thirty.

"Fine. I don't care about the other stuff. But, um, can you bring your costume? Because you'll need to dress as Robin Hood."

He glanced over at me, his jaw muscles tight. "You want me to pull up to your house wearing a blond wig, a tunic, and green tights?"

"Jeremy is in first grade. He doesn't realize you're an actor. He thinks you're really Robin Hood."

"This just keeps getting better." Steve swung the trailer door open. I followed him.

The first thing Steve did when we got inside was phone his personal assistant and explain the situation to him. He came to the trailer right away. Steve introduced him as Ron Bosco, and called him Ron while they talked, but it was clear from the moment he stepped inside that everyone else called him Mr. Bosco. The man was all seriousness. In fact, he may have been a calculator in a former life. I got the sense that his entire existence consisted of rows and columns of numbers.

Mr. Bosco eyed me over, clearly displeased, then stepped into the kitchenette with Steve and gave him a hushed lecture about why this was a bad idea. Steve kept saying, "I know, I know, but I made a promise. I'll come back as soon as I can."

Mr. Bosco opened his laptop and insisted on checking the internet to see if it would be faster to take a plane to Las Vegas and drive to Henderson, which it wasn't. And besides, Steve didn't want to have to deal with the crowds at the airport. Mr. Bosco then checked into renting a charter plane, which was even more complicated and expensive, but he couldn't get a hold of anyone at the company he wanted, and wasn't sure when they'd return his message. Still, he thought the best idea was to charter a plane tomorrow after work and try to fit it in before the awards ceremony.

Steve vetoed that idea since they hadn't been able to get a hold of the plane company, and besides he thought that would be cutting things too close. He didn't want to be late for the awards ceremony.

I responded to this by obsessively looking at the clock and biting all of my fingernails off. Mr. Bosco wasted a half an hour trying to save Steve time. Finally Steve walked away from the computer and said it would be simpler to just drive there right now.

When Mr. Bosco had resigned himself to the fact that he couldn't talk Steve out of going with me, he eyed me over again, this time with a sour expression, then had me sign a nondisclosure form. I'm serious. He had the paperwork in his briefcase. It basically said I would never talk to any tabloids or reporters about anything Steve said or did in my presence. I also could not sue him for any reason.

How paranoid do you have to be to carry those sorts of papers around?

Steve called the wardrobe department and asked them to bring him a new Robin Hood costume. I also asked them to bring my clothes over, since I'd shoved them into a corner of the wardrobe trailer when I'd changed into a medieval dress.

Steve went into the back room to pack a travel bag and change into regular clothes, but before he left, he told me to wait in the living room. "Ron will keep you company," he said.

In a voice I wasn't supposed to hear, he said to Ron, "Don't let her get into trouble, and whatever you do, don't make any bets with her—especially ones involving archery or Rock, Paper, Scissors."

A lady from wardrobe came over with Steve's costume but reported that someone had found my clothes earlier, figured they were Esme's, and sent them out with the other dirty laundry to be dry-cleaned. She said she'd have them mailed to my house when they came back.

To tell you the truth, I didn't mind wearing Steve's clothes. I sort of liked his lucky poker shirt.

Before we left—and by this time it was almost four-thirty—Mr. Bosco gave Steve a wad of cash. Television stars apparently don't go to the ATM themselves; that is the sort of thing their personal assistants do for them. The money was for gas and food. I felt bad Steve had to pay for anything, but my purse was with Madison, and Steve had already rejected my offer to drive him to Nevada in my minivan. His exact words were, "I've got to meet Karli at five, and I'm not pulling up to the restaurant in a minivan with two teenage girls and an assortment of wildlife."

He had tried to call Karli to cancel, but she didn't pick up her cell phone, and he didn't want to stand her up. He told me he'd just stop by the restaurant and tell her he couldn't stay.

I tried to give him the money the security guards had given me to pay for the gas, but he had looked at me incredulously, like I'd insulted him. "I'm not taking your money. Not now. Not ever."

During Mr. Bosco's investigation of flight times, I'd called Madison and told her she could head home because I'd be traveling with Steve. It wasn't that I really wanted to spend time with Mr. I-must-have-a-nondisclosure-form-before-you-can-hang-out-with-me. I just thought it would be too easy for him to break his promise if I wasn't there in the car with him.

Madison was all concerned about me going off on a four-hour car trip with a stranger, although mostly she was concerned I wouldn't be able to find my way home. I had to assure her that Steve's BlackBerry had GPS and he'd already programmed my address into it.

"Call me every once in a while so I know where you are," she'd said, and then added, "Oh, wait, I have your cell phone charger in my car. Is your battery about to run out? Does Steve have a phone?"

"We'll be fine," I told her. But after I hung up with her, I turned off my cell phone to conserve the battery.

As it turned out, we didn't actually take Steve's car. Steve, like most of the cast, had a driver that chauffeured him to the set, so he borrowed one of the studio's cars, a beige BMW. Apparently this is one of the perks of being a star: You can borrow expensive vehicles on a moment's notice.

At first Steve didn't say anything as we drove. I figured he was ticked off about having to do this favor for me, so I listened to the radio and didn't say anything either. We were nearly in Beverly Hills before Steve told me again that he'd make his meeting with Karli as short as possible.

"I thought you and Karli broke up," I said.

"We did. I'm mostly picking up some books she borrowed."

I turned in my seat and looked at him. "Really? What sort of books?"

He glanced at me. "Are you surprised I read?"

"No, I'm surprised she does."

He sent me a questioning gaze.

"Well, people who record videos of themselves rolling around in the sand with an entire platoon of lifeguards generally aren't very literary."

"Lifeguards don't come in platoons."

"You didn't answer my question about the books."

He looked out at traffic and not at me. "History books, mostly."

"Impressive. I take back everything I said about her."

The corners of his mouth lifted. "Well, it might have been impressive if she ever read them, but she didn't."

I smiled because I'd been right. "I'm still impressed you read them."

"Don't be. I started reading up on the Middle Ages to prepare for my role, then found I liked history." He glanced down at the car clock and grimaced. It read five o'clock. "I'm going to be ten minutes late."

"Sorry." I felt a stab of guilt for taking him away, and then a worse thought came to me. "You were trying to work things out with her, weren't you?"

He turned to look at me. "No. Why would you think that?"

"Usually if you've broken up with someone and then you want to get together with them for dinner, there are ulterior motives."

He shook his head. "Not this time. In fact, she's the one who suggested we meet for dinner."

"Oh, no." I put my fingers over my mouth. "That's even worse. She wants to get back together with you, and I'm ruining it."

His eyebrows drew together. "No, she's just returning my books. It's a friendly, clear-the-air sort of dinner."

This didn't relieve my guilt, as he was obviously ignorant about how women tried to recapture men. "You could offer to bring her with us. On the drive you'd have plenty of time to reconnect."

"We're not reconnecting," he said firmly. "You shouldn't jump to conclusions." And then he didn't say much for the rest of the drive to the restaurant.

Every once in a while I sneaked a look at him, at his tan hands resting on the steering wheel, his muscled arms, his faultless profile. It seemed unfair to the rest of humanity that his features should be so perfect. It was especially annoying to me because my mind kept drifting in that direction and then it was hard to think about anything else. His looks could intoxicate even a rational girl, and the last thing I needed was to start having a crush on a guy I would never see again after a few hours.

I made myself look out the window and stop glancing at him. He didn't seem to notice.

We pulled up to the Holland Grill, a quaint sidewalk café with baskets of hanging flowers, large shuttered windows, and music drifting out onto the sidewalk. Several couples ate on a large patio, which was surrounded by a picket fence. Tablecloths fluttered in the breeze. It was a perfectly romantic setting, and I wondered if Karli had chosen the location.

Cars lined the road in front of the restaurant, so Steve parked on the other side of the street a little way down. Before he shut the door, he turned back toward me with serious eyes. "Don't get out of the car. I'll try to make this fast."

I leaned toward him. "At least reschedule with her so she knows you're not blowing her off."

"We are not reconnecting." As he shut the car door, he tilted his head down and gave me a half smile. "While you're waiting, you can work on that whole jumping-to-conclusions thing we talked about."

He turned away from me and strode across the street.

I watched him and had to admit he had a nice walk. Confident. Masculine. Poor Karli. I bet when she saw him she wished she had never broken up with him.

Karli stood waiting in front of the restaurant. I hadn't noticed her at first because she wore sunglasses and, well, because she wore normal clothes—jeans and a blouse—as opposed to the black leather miniskirt and fishnet stockings sort of thing she'd taken to wearing since her last CD came out.

As Steve approached, Karli slipped her sunglasses on top of her head and smiled at him. She walked toward him, and when they met she took hold of his hand and kissed him on the cheek. When she finished kissing him, she didn't let go of his hand. They stood talking, and her gaze ran up and down him. Her body language wasn't so much friendly as sultry. Plus, she wasn't carrying any books.

And he accused me of jumping to conclusions. Men can be so clueless at times. I turned away from the two of them, and that's when I saw a photographer hiding behind a convertible two cars in front of me.

I was pretty sure Steve—Mr. Nondisclosure, Mr. We're Just Having a Friendly Dinner—wouldn't appreciate this violation of his privacy. So I did the first thing that came to mind. I hit the horn.

This got Steve's attention. He looked over at our car. I used exaggerated arm motions to point ahead of me. Even from as far away as I sat, I saw his eyes turn cold, as though I'd overstepped my boundaries. He turned back to Karli with a shrug, like he didn't know who I was.

Well, that was gratitude for you.

Unfortunately, it wasn't just Steve who had seen my

hand motions, so had the photographer. Now he turned his camera on me. I slunk down in the seat, but that only encouraged him to come closer.

I noticed he wasn't the only photographer around. I saw one behind a tree. Another sat at a table on the patio, but ever so casually took pictures of Karli holding Steve's hand.

The photographer from down the street came right up to the BMW, his camera clicking in my direction. With his telephoto lens, I was pretty sure he could get a picture of the fillings in my teeth if I opened my mouth to say anything. He alternated his pictures of me with pictures of Karli, who now stood seductively close to Steve, her hand on his arm and her face raised in a pout.

I opened the car door, slammed it shut, and hurried across the street. Even as I walked up, Steve still faced Karli. He didn't even acknowledge he knew me. I went and stood right beside him. Karli sent me a scathing look, as though I had no right to approach them. Which is when I stopped feeling sorry for her.

"I hate to interrupt you," I said, "but the reason I tried to get your attention earlier was to tell you there are photographers all over the place." I motioned behind me. "See? There's one right over there by the car."

Steve's head spun around, for the first time taking in the cameras. At this point, they had all come out of hiding. One walked around the side of the building toward us, so close I could hear his shutter clicking.

Karli narrowed her eyes at me. "Who is this girl, and why is she with you?" Then she let out a gasp and took a step back. "And why is she wearing your clothes?"

She said this too loudly. The clicking of the shutters increased.

Steve grabbed hold of my arm, but kept his gaze on Karli. His expression darkened, and his voice dropped. "Where did all of these photographers come from? You set this up, didn't you?"

Karli's eyes glittered and she lifted her chin. "What if I did? It's no more than you deserve. I can't believe you broke off our dinner date while another girl waited for you in your car!" Her hand tightened into a fist, like she wanted to hit him—or me, but instead she turned on her heel and stormed away.

I didn't have time to see where she went because Steve took hold of my elbow and pulled me back across the street. The photographers preserved every footstep we took on film.

"Who's your new girlfriend?" one of them called out.

"Don't say anything," Steve said to me.

I didn't. I couldn't.

"What's your name?" the photographer called to me again.

Another one added, "Where did you meet?"

They stood in our way of getting to the car. Steve stopped in front of them but still held on to my arm. I wondered if he thought they might grab me away from him.

"Move away from my car," he told them.

But they didn't move, and the photographer that had been at the restaurant came up behind us. I felt surrounded, trapped. "Why did you come here to meet Karli if you've got another girlfriend?" he asked.

"Does Esme know about this?"

"Are those really your clothes she's wearing?"

The photographer from the tree had joined the others. "How old are you?" He took another photo of me, and lowered his camera. "You don't look older than fourteen."

I let out an insulted gasp. "I'm seventeen."

Steve flinched, and I remembered I wasn't supposed to say anything. He said, "She's just a friend. Now, would you all mind getting away from my car. We're about to go visit with her family."

They still didn't move. The sidewalk felt claustrophobic.

"If she's just a friend, why is she wearing your clothes?"

Steve didn't answer. Instead he turned and pulled me

through the group back across the street and to the restaurant.

We went inside. The smell of food engulfed me, but didn't make me feel hungry. My stomach had tightened into a ball of nerves while I'd been jostled by the photographers. Steve asked the hostess if we could have a private room to make a phone call. Without questioning him, she led us to an office and told him to let her know if he needed anything else. She fluttered her eyelashes and smiled at him as she said this.

Only after the door shut did Steve let go of my arm. He pulled out his cell phone and glared at me. "Two minutes," he said. "I can't believe you didn't last two minutes before you told a group of reporters you were seventeen."

"I don't really look fourteen, do I?"

"No." He pressed speed dial and held the phone to his ear. "That guy tricked you into telling him how old you were and you fell for it. Now they're all going to report that—" The call went through and he stopped midsentence and started a new conversation.

"Hello, Sergeant Garcia, this is Steve Raleigh. I'm down at the Holland Grill, and I have so many photographers blocking my car I can't get to it. Can you send an officer down to clear them out?" A short pause followed, then Steve said, "Great. I really appreciate it."

He said good-bye, flipped the phone shut, and slipped it back into his pocket.

"You have the police on your speed dial?" I asked.

He let out a grunt. "And you wouldn't believe how often it comes in handy." He went to the window and peered through one of the slits in the shutters. I stared at his profile, tracing the lines of his face with my eyes. He really was impossibly handsome.

"Are they still there?" I asked.

"Oh, yeah, and on their cell phones." He put one hand to his temple as though he'd developed a headache. "Why couldn't you have stayed in the car like I asked you to?"

"Because you seem so worried about your privacy—I thought you'd want to know about the photographers. It didn't look like just a friendly meeting between you and Karli, by the way."

"Yeah, she had some other ideas."

"I told you she wanted you back." The words prickled me, although I knew they shouldn't. It shouldn't matter to me who he dated.

"More likely she wanted some publicity for her new album." He shook his head. "I should have suspected something when she wanted to meet for dinner at five o'clock. Anytime a celebrity wants to meet you outside when the lighting is at its best, be suspicious."

"It doesn't make sense." I considered Karli for a moment: the bitter breakup songs she'd written, the way she'd lured him to the restaurant and draped her arms around him, how she'd yelled at me and stomped off. "She's acting more like you broke up with her and not the other way around."

He didn't say anything, just looked out the window again.

And then it made sense. "You did break up with her, didn't you?"

He turned back to me and I could tell from his expression I'd been right. He shrugged instead of admitting it, though. "That doesn't matter. What matters now is if we're going to spend several hours together, you've got to do a better job of listening to me. In the future, if I tell you not to get out of the car, don't get out of the car."

"I wouldn't have had to if you paid attention to me when I tried to tell you about the paparazzi the first time."

"I thought you were telling me to hurry so we could go."

I walked over to the desk and sat down on the chair with a thud. "I wouldn't be that rude."

He laughed, but I didn't see what was funny, so I arched my eyebrows at him.

He leaned against the wall and surveyed me. "You sneaked into a stadium and the studio lot, you pretended to be people you weren't, brought a snake into a place with horses, broke out of my trailer, and stole my lucky poker shirt—but you're offended that I might think you're rude?"

I leaned back in the chair and folded my arms. "There is a difference between being determined and being rude."

He laughed again.

"You out of all people should understand. Sometimes you have to take matters into your own hands. I'm just doing what Robin Hood would have done."

The amusement didn't leave his face. "Which is why many characters on the show want to string Robin Hood up."

"Don't give me a hard time. You'd do the exact same thing if it meant helping your little brother."

His expression momentarily tensed, and I remembered he was estranged from his family.

I tried to soften my last statement. "I mean, if you had a little brother. I don't know if you do."

"I do," he said. "He's your age."

"Oh." The room grew awkwardly quiet. It seemed like I should say something else. "Are you close?"

"We used to be, but my family lives in Apple Valley now." He must have seen my blank look because he added, "It's about ninety miles away, so I don't see him much anymore."

Ninety miles didn't seem that far away, but I didn't press the point.

After a few more minutes, a police car arrived and the paparazzi scattered. We walked back to the car, this time without Steve guiding me by the arm.

I shouldn't have missed it, but I did.

Chapter 12

We pulled away from the restaurant and made our way through the streets of Beverly Hills. Almost immediately, we hit rush-hour traffic. And not the normal rush-hour traffic I was used to. We hit insane, there-are-way-too-many-people-in-California traffic. It took us more than an hour to make it through LA and then it was stop-and-go all along I-15.

While we crept along the road, Steve asked me about Jeremy and what he expected Robin Hood to do. So I talked about Jeremy for a while. Then I alternated between staring at the cars around us, staring at the speedometer, and waiting for the digital clock to switch numbers: 6:37 . . . 6:38. . . .

"Tell me more about Jeremy," Steve said.

"Why?"

"Because you only relax when you talk about him.

I'm afraid if we spend much more time in traffic you'll completely claw your armrest apart."

"I couldn't possibly claw anything," I said. "I bit off all my fingernails in your trailer." Still, I told him more about Jeremy. I went on for over an hour. It all spilled out, even things I wouldn't normally have told a stranger, like my trip to Toys "R" Us and the guy in the leather jacket who'd chased me through the store.

That part made Steve smile. "The poor slob. He didn't know who he was up against—the incarnation of Robin Hood as a teenage girl."

Finally I said, "I've done enough talking. It's your turn. Why don't you tell me something about yourself."

He kept his eyes on the road. "I thought you already knew everything about me. Two Broadway shows, three movies, a toothpaste commercial—"

"I'm sure a few things have escaped my attention."

"Probably not. I'm not that interesting."

After spilling my guts to him, this felt like a splash of cold water. It was as though he'd told me we were still strangers or, worse yet, that he didn't trust me. Which, now that I thought about it, was probably the case. I'd never given him a reason to trust me.

I looked out the window. "I suppose not."

"You suppose I'm not that interesting?" he said.

"I'm only agreeing with you. I thought celebrities expected that sort of treatment."

A grin slid across his face. "Now I'm the typical egomaniac TV star?"

"Well, how would I know any differently if you won't say anything about yourself?"

He glanced my way, contemplating me. "How did you know I was the one who broke up with Karli?"

I didn't know why he was taking this conversational detour. I shrugged at him. "I could tell by the way she looked at you."

"And you knew Karli wanted more than just dinner before I even pulled up to the restaurant. How did you know that?"

I shrugged again. "I'm a girl. I know how girls think." Especially when hot guys were involved.

He gave me a penetrating look. "*That* is why I don't want to tell you anything about myself. Do you know what I know about you, Annika? You're the type of girl who gets whatever she wants. You smile and doors open for you, but if that doesn't work, you're not above manipulating people and events. I know the type. Karli was the same way."

I opened my mouth to protest, but he held up his hand. "I'm not saying I don't admire your confidence, because I do. But the thing is, I can already tell you're smarter than Karli and more intuitive than most people, and that worries me. I'm in the car with a smarter, more cunning version of Karli. You'd be cautious about what you said about yourself too."

I leaned back against the seat. "I'm not sure whether to feel complimented or insulted."

"And you're only seventeen . . . ," he said to himself.

"You're only nineteen," I pointed out.

"Yeah, but nine of those years have been spent in Hollywood. Hollywood years are like dog years, so I'm really—"

"Seventy-three."

"And you can do math problems in your head." He let out a sigh. "I'm not saying another word around you."

"Why? Are you hiding something?"

He smiled. "Of course I am. Everybody hides things. I bet you're hiding things too."

I ran my fingers through my hair. "I'll tell you a confession if you'll tell me one."

He nodded as though considering it. "Okay."

"I can't really cry on demand. That was a total lie. I actually don't cry at all."

I thought it would make him laugh, but instead his eyebrows drew together. "That isn't healthy."

"Right. I'll add that to my list right behind driving too fast and draping snakes around my neck."

He smiled, but his eyes were intent. "I think you're the kind of person who refuses to take things seriously."

This from a guy who made a living wearing tights. "I take some things seriously. I take Jeremy's illness seriously."

He glanced at me, reading me like he might have read a passing sign. "Yes, you do. And you're used to plowing over obstacles to get what you want. It must be hard for you to finally run into something you can't control."

"I don't need to control it," I said. "I just need to find a way to tip the odds in my brother's favor." I was lying, though. I needed to control it. I needed to win this time more than I had ever needed to win anything. To change the subject, I said, "So what's your confession?"

He eyed me over, and I could tell he was debating what to say. Finally he turned back to the road. "My confession is I'm intuitive too."

"That's a confession?"

"I didn't have to tell you. I could have gone on figuring out stuff about you without warning you."

Which made me feel as though he had just confessed to reading my mind. "What exactly do you mean when you say 'intuitive'?"

"Intuitive means you can tell things about people, you know, like when they're lying to you."

"Oh, you mean like when you confessed to being intuitive, but I could tell that wasn't your original confession. You meant to say something else and then changed your mind."

He moved in his seat uncomfortably. "Right. Like that."

"What were you going to say?"

"That I'm hungry. I think I'll get off at this exit, fill up the car, and buy something to eat."

"Oh, see—I can tell you're lying."

"No, I'm actually hungry. It's almost eight."

I put my hand on the back of his seat and leaned closer to him. "Come on, what were you going to say?"

But he didn't even glance at me. He pulled off at the exit to Barstow, looked at his GPS, and told me we still had about 150 miles to go. Two hours. Then he said, "So, you never told me—do your parents know where you are?"

"Well, no. I sort of forgot to tell them." I'd meant to call my parents when I'd first left the city with Steve. It was okay to tell them what I'd done now because Steve had agreed to come with me. They couldn't yell at me for going off on some wild goose chase when I was bringing the goose back to meet Jeremy.

I pulled my phone out of my pocket and turned it on. I'd missed three messages from my parents. I listened to them while Steve found a gas station. First I heard my mother's voice telling me to come home. In the second message she sounded more frantic, asking where I was and why hadn't I called. Didn't I realize the last thing my parents needed right now was for me to disappear and not answer my phone? It was irresponsible of me, and we were going to have a long talk about my behavior when I got home.

The third message had been left only minutes ago. It was my father using his forced calm voice, which meant my mother was too upset to speak with me. He said he had spoken with Madison's parents and knew about our road trip to California. He thought it was the most foolish thing I'd ever done in my life, and he couldn't believe it of me. Didn't I realize the danger I'd put myself in, that I'd put Madison in? Didn't I realize the inconvenience I'd caused for Steve Raleigh? Was it really worth all of that so Jeremy could meet someone he saw on TV? Jeremy would have been just as happy with a trip to see Santa at the mall. Dad added that he wanted me to call right away.

While Steve pulled up in front of the gas station and shut off the car, I lay my phone in my lap and felt sick. I had really thought Dad would understand. A part of me even thought he'd be proud of me for doing something this big for Jeremy.

Steve opened the car door but turned back to face me. "I'm going to get something to eat. Do you want anything?"

"I'm not hungry."

"You should eat something anyway." He looked at the phone on my lap, then back at my face. "Come on, you knew your parents would be angry."

"Maybe I'm not as intuitive as you thought."

He smiled, but his eyes were serious. "You knew—otherwise, you would have told them before now."

I watched him walk into the gas station, but not even the sight of his broad shoulders and faded jeans could take my mind off the impending phone call.

I speed-dialed home. Jeremy picked up after about two seconds. He said, "Annika, where are you?"

"I'm driving back to Nevada. And, hey, I talked to my genie about your Teen Robin Hood wish. You'll get that soon—before you go in for surgery."

Instead of being excited, his voice brimmed with reproach. "Mom and Dad are really worried about you. Mom cried at dinner."

Great.

I heard the phone being taken away from Jeremy and then Leah's voice. "You realize you're in a boatload of trouble, don't you?"

"Yeah."

Her voice dropped to a whisper. "Did you actually drive all the way to California to try and find Steve Raleigh?"

"Yeah, he's with me right now."

"Steve Raleigh is with you?" I could hear the doubt in her voice. "*The* Steve Raleigh?"

No, some random Steve Raleigh I found wandering around the street. Honestly, Leah refuses to believe that I am a competent person. In her mind I will always be perpetually thirteen years old. "Yes," I told her. "He's driving back to Henderson with me."

"Uh-huh." Still doubt. "Can I talk to him?"

"Well, he's not actually with me this second. He's inside the gas station buying something for dinner."

"Ahh. Of course. Because celebrities eat at gas stations all the time."

"It really is him." I didn't get to say more because my father took a hold of the phone.

He asked where I was, whether I was okay, and then laid into me, repeating everything he'd already said in his message, but with a harsher tone this time. This trip of mine was *irresponsible*, *dangerous*, and I'd *lied* to them about where I was going.

But I couldn't stop thinking that he was just like Leah. He was mad because he still thought of me as thirteen years old. "I'm sorry I lied to you about all of this," I said. "But I had to try and help Jeremy, and I knew you wouldn't let me go otherwise."

"Of course we wouldn't have let you go. You're never to go anywhere, *anywhere* without getting our permission first." He said a lot after that, but my mind kept circling around those phrases. I realized that my parents had been holding on to Jeremy so fervently, they'd tightened their grip on me too. And perhaps I was just as guilty of clinging to them. But no matter what happened with Jeremy, I had to grow up and make decisions—even bad ones, for myself. I already had.

I said, "Dad, I'm going away to college in less than a year. Can't you trust my judgment a little? I pulled off this impossible thing to help Jeremy. Can't you be happy about that?"

There was a long pause. When he spoke again his voice sounded softer. "Look, I understand that Jeremy's cancer has been hard on you. Maybe harder than your mother and I realized. I know we haven't been giving you the attention that you need." I wasn't sure what he meant by that, but I was afraid he was implying this trip had been part of some nervous breakdown. I wondered what Madison had told them.

"We'll be there in two hours," I said. "Let Jeremy stay up until Steve and I come, because Steve's going to turn around and drive back to California afterward."

My dad grumbled about this, said to call him when we hit Nevada, then added again that we'd have a long talk about this when I got home. Which I wasn't looking forward to. I snapped the phone shut and slipped it into my pocket.

Steve came back out of the store and handed me a

bottled water, a muffin, a yogurt, and a plastic spoon. "It was the healthiest thing I could find."

I looked at him, but my mind stayed back on my father's conversation. How much of his anger was because he thought of me as a child? How thin was the line between a really good idea and a nervous breakdown?

"You haven't had dinner," Steve said. "You need to eat something."

I hadn't eaten since breakfast, but I wasn't hungry. When I still didn't move, he added, "I'm not starting the car again until I see food going into your mouth."

Which as far as threats went, was pretty effective. I opened the yogurt and took a spoonful. He gave me a satisfied look and went to pump the gas.

As I ate I watched him put the gas nozzle into the tank. Pumping gas was such an ordinary thing to do, it was hard to believe famous people ever did it. While the gas ran, he took a squeegee and wiped off the front window.

I glanced at the cars around us, wondering if any of them had noticed him. Everyone seemed oblivious except for one gray car. A man stood pumping gas, but his gaze kept returning to Steve.

I had seen that gray car behind us in the thick of traffic. I peered closer at the man, and my stomach clenched. I'd seen him at the restaurant too. He'd been the one who said I looked fourteen. He must be following us.

As Steve put the squeegee back, he took out his PDA and pushed buttons on it. I tried to get his attention, but he only looked at the PDA and not me. I would have gotten out of the car and told him, but my last trip out of the car in front of photographers had not gone well.

Besides, if Steve knew we had paparazzi trailing us, would he call the police again? How long would that delay us this time?

I stayed where I was, and in another minute Steve put the nozzle back on the pump and opened the passenger side door.

"Jim just e-mailed me my new lines. Do you mind driving while I go over them?"

"That's fine." I slid over to the driver's seat and he got in the passenger side, still reading off of his PDA.

When I pulled out of the gas station, so did the gray car. I headed onto the freeway, every once in a while glancing in the rearview mirror. The car kept its distance, but its headlights never lagged far behind us.

Steve ate and read. I went over my options. How did one lose a car on the freeway? I continued to increase my speed. The gray car kept pace.

Steve chuckled. "Jim now has Maid Marion crawling

out the window of Sir Guy's castle and leaping into a tree. I wonder how Esme will like that?"

"Does she get pushed into a fishpond anywhere in the story?"

Steve shook his head. "Not that I can see."

"Too bad. I suggested that plot twist too."

Steve looked at the speedometer for the first time. "You're going ninety-five. If you get pulled over going twenty-five miles over the speed limit, it's a criminal offense."

"Really? How do you know that?"

Steve smiled. "Don't ask. Just slow down a little."

"I'm trying to lose that car behind us. It's one of the guys from the restaurant."

"What?" Steve's head swung backward to check. "Where?" But I didn't have to point it out. He saw it and swore.

"I recognized him at the gas station. It's the guy who thinks I look fourteen."

Steve ran his fingers through his hair and looked back at the car again.

I asked, "How do you usually get rid of them when they follow you?"

"Usually I don't give them interesting enough stories that they want to trail me for hours on end."

"You must have some method for discouraging them," I prompted.

"Yeah, I drive home and sit in my house until they get tired and go away."

"Well, we just need to think of something else. Come on, what would Robin Hood do?"

Steve lifted one hand in exasperation. "Shoot him? Steal all of his stuff and give it to poor Saxon villagers. . . ."

I rolled my eyes. "Fine. If you aren't going to be any help, I'll take care of it myself." I slowed my speed way down.

"This is the fast lane," Steve said. "Is your plan to annoy the other drivers until they—"

But he didn't finish because at that point I veered the car onto the median that divided the highway so we could head back the opposite direction. And let me say, for a guy who can do his own stunts, you wouldn't have expected him to grab hold of the dashboard and curse like a sailor as we drove over to the other side. I mean, okay, so we flattened a bush and some branches flew into the windshield. I could still see. And besides, bushes are resilient. It would grow back eventually.

We jiggled and bumped over the gravel to the other side. I glanced at the rearview mirror and didn't see any headlights following us across the median. "Did we lose him?"

Steve still had hold of the dashboard as though he

expected it to jump in his lap. "I can't believe you just did that! Are you crazy?"

I gripped the steering wheel tighter. "Why do people keep asking me that?"

He turned to stare at me, his eyes worried. "Who else keeps asking you that? Are any of them doctors?"

I put my foot down on the accelerator, heading the wrong way but getting there really fast. I needed a place to get off the freeway to turn around. "I am not crazy. Because at least when I have crazy things happen to me, I know they're crazy. Crazy people would think they're normal."

Steve still had one hand on the dashboard. "You're not reassuring me at all. Pull over and let me drive."

"I'll pull over at the next exit."

It turned out the next exit was at Barstow, eight miles back the way we came—and driving eighty miles an hour there and then back again added twelve minutes to the trip. I really am pretty good at math problems.

Steve didn't speak the entire way there. He just kept tapping his fingers on the door handle, as though calculating his chances of survival should he need to fling open the door and jump.

Finally I pulled over to the shoulder of the road and put the car in park. I didn't get out. I was half afraid if I did he would lock the doors and take off.

Steve leaned back in his seat and watched me, his expression serious. "So exactly what sort of crazy things have happened to you?"

I kept my hands on the steering wheel and didn't answer.

He reached over, pulled the key out of the ignition, and leaned back in his seat again. "I don't mind sitting here. You're the one who's in a hurry. What time does Jeremy go to bed, anyway?"

"That's blackmail," I said.

"That's what Robin Hood would do."

I let my head fall back against the seat in defeat. "Okay, come around to the driver's side, and I'll talk while you drive."

He did. Although he drove slowly at first. He wanted to make sure the gray car hadn't pulled over to the side of the road somewhere, waiting for us to drive by so it could resume tailing us. This added more time to the trip, but I didn't have the heart to calculate how much. Stupid paparazzi.

"Talk," Steve told me.

My foot immediately began to twitch. I made it stop. "Last night I dreamt that the Grim Reaper came to our house . . . and today sometimes it feels like the dream didn't end, like he's still here, watching me."

Steve shrugged. "Some nightmares are that way. That's not crazy."

"In your trailer, it felt like the Grim Reaper leaned over my shoulder and told me that Jeremy and I couldn't escape from the underworld." I rubbed my forehead, trying to make the memory go away. "When a person is being followed around by the Grim Reaper—well, either I'm sliding toward insanity, or this has bad omen written all over it."

Steve's attention drifted from the road to my face, but he showed no shock at my confession, just concern. After a moment, he looked back at the road. "How long has it been since you've had a good night's sleep?"

"I don't remember."

"How much sleep did you get last night?"

"Four hours. Maybe five."

Steve's voice turned soft, caressing. His warm brown eyes flickered to mine again. "It's not insanity or a bad omen. When you're under a lot of stress and sleep deprived, things can happen to your mind." As though offering up proof, he said, "My father used to be a policeman in LA. He had to deal with all sorts of bad things—murders, gangs, drug dealers. Once when he was trying to break up a fight, he got stabbed. While he was home recovering, it all came back to him—every violent crime scene he'd ever gone to was suddenly right in front of him, like a slide show."

I drew my breath in sharply, and Steve went on, trying to reassure me. "It only happened once. And he'd heard about this sort of thing from other police officers, so he wasn't even too worried about it. My point is, you're going through a hard time right now. It wouldn't be normal if you didn't fall apart a little."

That made sense, but part of me couldn't shake the feeling that the Grim Reaper was real, a living being, watching me, just outside my peripheral vision. Maybe a good night's rest would take care of that. Certainly after the surgery had gone well, everything would return to normal. And now that Steve was with me, I really thought things would work out.

Everything was looking up.

But half an hour outside of Barstow, in the middle of the Mojave Desert, the car broke down.

Chapter 13

*A*t first the car slowed down. Steve kept pressing the gas, but the car limped along, losing speed.

"This is bad," he said.

The engine light came on, and he steered the car over to the side of the road, where it rolled to a stop. He turned the ignition off and got out. I followed him, even though my entire knowledge of car mechanics consists of where to put in the gas. The night air bit into my bare legs, and I hugged my arms across my chest.

He lifted the hood and poked at things.

"What's wrong with it?" I asked.

"I don't know." More poking at things. "Whatever it is, I'm going to have to call a tow truck."

My first thought as I looked around in the darkness was: Why does God hate me?

Which was probably a foolish thought. God had better things to do than sabotage Steve's car. But still.

Steve took out a long, thin metal strip from the engine. "Our transmission fluid is gone. We must have broken a line when we went over the median. It's all leaked out."

Which made me feel even worse. It hadn't been God's vengeance. It had been me, driving the car like a maniac over shrubbery.

Steve called directory assistance and then made a phone call to a towing company back in Barstow. "Nothing to do now but wait," he said. "It's going to take them about a half an hour, forty-five minutes." Which meant it would be between nine and nine-fifteen when they got here, and then another half-hour trip back into Barstow where hopefully we could find a rental car.

I called my parents and explained what happened—well, minus the part about me cutting across a median. "Tell Jeremy we'll wake him up when we get there."

I shivered as I got back in the BMW. Steve turned on the car heater but also pulled his jacket from the backseat and gave it to me.

"Don't you want to wear it?" I asked him.

"You're only wearing shorts and a T-shirt. Besides, this way you have the complete Steve Raleigh clothing line."

"Thanks." I put on the jacket, enjoying the smell of Steve that clung to it, a sort of mellow woodsy smell. I tried not to let him see me snuggling into it so I could get deeper whiffs. Finally, I leaned my head against the seat and looked over at him. "Despite the way you yelled at me earlier and, you know, had me dragged off by security guards—you're actually a nice guy."

Even in the dark I could see his eyes glittering and his trademark smirk. "Thanks." He looked at me for a moment longer. "And you're seventeen."

"Right. I haven't had a birthday since the last time you pointed my age out." I knew he was telling me I was too young for him, and it irked me. I wasn't too young, and he shouldn't have just assumed that I was attracted to him. Even if I was.

I leaned away from him and kept my voice casual to show that I didn't care. "What was your first confession— the one you didn't tell me?"

"I'm still not going to tell you."

"You owe me a confession, then. It's only fair. I've already told you things about myself no one else knows."

He cocked his head at me. "Is this some sort of game girls play at slumber parties? Why do you want to poke around in my psyche?"

"I'm bored. What else are we going to do in a broken-down car in the middle of nowhere?"

He raised an eyebrow, and I blushed, realizing how that had sounded. A wicked glint flashed through his expression. "See, that's why I pointed out that you're only seventeen. Seventeen-year-olds are still naïve."

"I'm not naïve, and you're only two years older than me."

He sat further away from me and ignored my last statement. "Why don't we save time, and instead of me trying to come up with a confession you're satisfied with, you can just ask me whatever it is you want to know."

I wanted to ask about his family. I wanted to know why he'd sued to be an adult at sixteen years old, but that felt too personal. "Tell me about Karli. I have a hard time picturing the two of you together."

He looked up at the car ceiling and rubbed his fingers over his chin. "I'm not sure that's a good subject."

"Too painful?"

"No. If I talk about her, then you'll realize I'm not such a nice guy after all."

"Because you broke her heart?"

"Because I went out with her for the wrong reasons in the first place."

"And what were those reasons?"

He returned his gaze to me, but I could tell he was still reluctant. Finally he said, "I've worked in this business my entire life. I don't remember a time when my mother wasn't hauling me around to auditions. I even made some good money as a kid. But nobody knew who I was until *Robin Hood* became a hit. Before then, I doubt Karli would have paused long enough to give me an autograph, let alone give me her phone number. I dated her because I could. Because that meant I'd arrived. I had a girlfriend that thousands of guys wanted." He looked at me again. "Do you still think I'm a nice guy?"

I reached out and put my hand on his knee. "Yes. Because you knew it was wrong. That's why you broke up with her."

"Well, that and because she really started to get on my nerves. She had this obsessive need to primp. I still can't walk by a mirror without feeling like I should pull someone away from it."

He didn't move my hand off of his knee, but I saw him looking at it. His voice was soft, lulling. "We've only known each other for one day."

"I realize that."

His gaze stayed on my hand. "You've never dealt with the tabloids. You have no idea what the paparazzi are like or how to avoid them." His voice slowed as he added to his list, "And you live in Nevada, which is a four-hour drive away."

I leaned closer to him. "Is there some reason you keep bringing up these little facts?"

Now his gaze moved to mine, dazzling and intense.

"I'm reminding myself why it would never work out between us, because I don't want to do anything stupid."

He was probably right, but at the moment I wasn't thinking intelligently. Or cautiously. I never would have come to California if I hadn't been beyond all of that. I leaned over and kissed him.

I hadn't expected him to kiss me back, but he did. He put his hand against my cheek and layered soft kisses around my mouth. He kissed me like I was fragile and he didn't want to break me.

I had kissed other guys, but it had never made me so nervous before. He pulled me closer to him, and I worried he'd feel the pulse of my heart beating against my chest like a frightened bird. But I wasn't frightened. I just couldn't believe this was happening. I'd seen this guy ride across my TV screen, and now he sat here kissing me. I wanted to hold on to the moment so it could never pass away.

He leaned away from me and let out a ragged breath. "Any chance that when you graduate you'll go to college in California?"

"I've always liked UCLA."

He bent forward and kissed me again, this time less softly. I wrapped my arms around his neck.

Then almost as quickly as he kissed me, he pushed me away from him, placing me back in my seat.

"This is a bad idea."

I blinked at him in confusion. "What?"

"You're vulnerable and you're tired. I don't take advantage of my fans."

I let out a slow breath. He was still close enough that he made me feel dizzy. "Okay, even though I woke up before dawn to buy an action figure that looked like you, technically, I'm not your fan."

He laughed, a rich sound that sent sparks up my spine. "That's what I like about you, Annika. You keep things in perspective."

I smiled back at him, trying to calm my rapid heartbeat. I needed to pretend my mind wasn't still spinning with the experience. I needed to pretend it wasn't a big deal to kiss him, or to be so soundly pushed away. I wanted to think of some casual retort, but couldn't.

His PDA had somehow fallen to the floor, and he picked it up. "I still need to run lines. Do you want to help me?"

And so we did. For the next hour—the tow truck driver had apparently been optimistic in how long it would take him to reach us—I read him his cues and listened as he said his lines, complete with facial expression and voice inflection. I probably would have laughed at his seriousness, except the whole time my mind lingered on our kiss, processing the implications. Had it meant anything to him?

Did I mean anything to him?

Would we ever see each other again after this?

He was probably used to girls throwing themselves at him, and I was just another in a long line of available teenage groupies. He wouldn't give me another thought once we parted.

I found this hard to grapple with, because somewhere in that kiss, my own feelings had emerged, vibrant and strong. Desperately strong. As he said lines to me, I could barely concentrate on his words. I kept getting lost in the curve of his jaw, the way his eyes had a power to speak on their own, and the movement of his lips.

I'd been able to talk to him so easily. I'd told him all about myself. Being with him made me feel as though everything would work out all right. I didn't want to give that up. I didn't want to go back to being alone again.

I had been counting down the minutes until we reached Henderson. Now I'd count them down for a different reason. I didn't want them to end.

We reached the climax of the script, where Robin Hood finally caught up with Maid Marion and she realized it was him and not Sir Guy's henchman following her. As she ran through the forest, he swooped down from a tree and grabbed her in his arms. At first she tried to fight him off, but then he called her name and she stopped struggling and threw her arms around him.

"Robin," I read to Steve, trying to mimic Maid Marion distressed-damsel voice the best I could, "it's you."

He gave me the Robin Hood grin. "Of course it's me. Did you forget I invited you to our May Day feast? You didn't think I'd let you avoid the invitation that easily, did you?"

"Oh, Robin . . . I thought that . . . and then . . . I was so afraid." It's this sort of dialogue that makes me want to slap Maid Marion, but I read the line anyway.

"You don't need to be afraid." He leaned closer to me, his voice intent yet tender. "You're stronger than you think."

I glanced up from the PDA. "That's not the line."

"What?"

"The line is: You don't need to be afraid, not as long as I have a say about it."

"It should be the other way," he said, and then I knew he was actually reading the line to me and not to Maid Marion. This should have made me feel better, but it didn't. I didn't want to be strong; I wanted to be comforted.

I looked back down at the PDA and waited for him to say his line the right way.

"What happens after that line?" he asked me.

I scanned through the stage directions. "You kiss Maid Marion."

He nodded as though adding it to a mental checklist. "You don't need to be afraid, not as long as I have a say about it."

Then he leaned over and kissed me.

I froze. For a moment, I wouldn't kiss him back. I didn't want to be a practice Maid Marion, and I refused to be just another available teenage groupie. But that only lasted for a moment; then I leaned into him. I was either stupid or in love. Probably both.

Headlights came up behind us, and we pulled away from each other. "How's that for timing?" Steve asked with a smile. He didn't wait for my answer before he opened his car door and stepped outside.

For a minute I sat in the car, staring ahead and trying to collect my thoughts. Then I followed after him. I had to. I didn't know where you were supposed to sit when they towed your car.

Steve and the tow truck driver stood by the truck. They were about the same height, but the driver was twice as wide. He shook his head, a tired baseball cap covering his graying ponytail. His belly bulged out over a pair of greasy-looking jeans, and all I could think was that Steve had better not make me sit next to this guy.

"It's fifty dollars to come out here and four dollars a mile after that." While the driver spoke, he chewed on something. I thought it was gum until he spit part of it out. Chewing tobacco. I bet the inside of his cab was a mess. "You got a credit card on you, kid?"

Steve handed him fifty dollars of his cash. "I have the money to pay you the rest, but not on me. I didn't bring my wallet with me, but when we get back to your shop, I'll have my personal assistant wire the rest to you."

The driver let out a snort. "Your personal assistant? Why not your fairy godmother? How old are you, kid?"

I walked up, but Steve didn't look at me. The driver did, though. His gaze ran over me in a way I didn't like.

Steve said, "I have the money. I'm Steve Raleigh."

The driver chewed his tobacco without showing any recognition.

"The actor," Steve said.

Still no recognition.

"You know, *Teen Robin Hood*."

The driver held his clipboard down and gave Steve the once over. "Right," he said without emotion. "I didn't recognize you without your Merry Men."

"So you know I'm good for the rest of the charge. Now if you can just take my car—"

The man let out a disgruntled sigh. "You got your name on the car registration?"

"Well, no, actually it's the studio's car—"

"And let me guess, you ain't got no driver's license, either?"

"Not with me."

The driver shoved Steve's bills into his pants pocket. "So what you're telling me is that you went joyriding around with your girlfriend in a car that ain't yours. You ran into trouble, and now you want a ride back to town, but it's been a busy night, and I got things to do besides wait around for the Sheriff of Nottingham to show up and tell me I got a stolen car on my hands. Too much paperwork."

Steve's words came out in a low growl. "It isn't stolen. I am who I say I am."

"He is," I added.

But the man turned and walked to his truck. "I seen the show advertised. Robin Hood's got blond hair."

"It's a wig!" I called out, but he'd already climbed in the cab and shut the door. I turned to Steve. "Why don't we—"

He held up a hand to cut me off. "No. We're not jumping on the back of the truck or whatever wild idea just entered your head." He took a hold of my arm as though to emphasize the point and keep me from flinging myself at passing vehicles. "I'm not actually Robin Hood, and neither are you. In real life, sometimes you've got to accept your setbacks."

"I was about to say, 'Why don't we get your costume out of the back of the car and prove it to him?'"

Steve let out a groan and dropped my arm, but it was

too late. The tow truck had already pulled away. Steve walked back to the car, muttering angrily. I followed after him, and we both climbed into the car.

"Where are the paparazzi when you need them?" he asked. "They show up at every special occasion and mundane event, but not when the tow truck driver doesn't recognize you."

I leaned back in my seat and pulled his jacket around me tighter. "Yeah, if one showed up now he could give us a ride."

It was nine-thirty. And we were still almost an hour and a half away from my house.

Steve picked up his PDA from the seat and turned it on. I glanced over to try and see what he was doing. "Are you calling another towing company? One of them is bound to be up on Hollywood's who's who."

"I'm calling who I should have called in the first place."

"Who?"

"My brother."

Chapter 14

The call was short, to the point, and when Steve hung up, I couldn't tell what his brother's reaction to the situation had been. Steve said, "My brother is calling a tow company, and he's driving out to switch cars with us. Unfortunately, it will be about forty minutes until either gets here. They're coming from Apple Valley."

"I thought you were estranged from your family."

"Just my parents. My brother and I still talk sometimes." His voice told me he'd left a lot unsaid, but I didn't press the point. "I have some e-mail to go through," he said. "Why don't you try to get some sleep. We've still got a long night ahead of us."

I knew I wouldn't be able to fall asleep. After all, it was only a little after nine-thirty, and I have a hard enough time falling asleep in my own bed. Still, I leaned the passenger seat way back and shut my eyes.

I liked being next to Steve. Hearing the movement of

his hands mixing in with the hum of the heater comforted me. He seemed so sturdy, so concrete. I shut my eyes and saw him in my mind as I'd seen him on TV so often, surrounded by the brilliance of trees and sunshine. He smiled with contagious confidence. As Robin Hood, he could do anything and knew everything.

I opened my eyes and saw his profile, handsome, perfect, and concentrating on his PDA.

"What do you think the purpose of life is?" I asked.

He glanced over at me, his eyes warm, but without the confidence of Robin Hood. "I don't know. Maybe it's different for each of us."

This was disappointing. The vision of Robin Hood standing all-knowing in the sunshine faded from my mind.

Steve's gaze flickered from his PDA to my face. "What do *you* think the purpose of life is?"

That was the problem. I didn't know anymore. "My Grandmother Truman used to say it was to make the world a better place. She said we're all given different gifts in order to help people. I always planned on becoming—I don't know—a defense lawyer or a detective or something, because I can figure people out so quickly. I thought that was the way I could make the world better."

"You don't believe that anymore?"

"Jeremy might never get the chance to use his gifts

to make the world better. Not everybody does. So how can that be the purpose of life?"

He didn't answer. His expression was unreadable in the darkness. Finally he said, "I don't have any answers for you. I'm not even a good role model. You want to use your talents to make the world a better place. I've only used mine to make money."

"Your acting makes people happy."

"I wasn't talking about acting. I take business classes when the show goes on hiatus. I've made some investments, and being able to figure people out quickly also helps during a deal. I know when people are being straight with me, when they'll go lower on their price—" He broke off his impromptu business lesson. "Maybe you're right. I'm not much like Robin Hood. I don't suppose Robin ever cared about interest rates or profit margins."

More to myself than to him, I said, "Why can't life turn out like it does on your show—neatly and with the good guys always winning in the end? Why can't stories be real?"

He reached over and moved a piece of hair away from my cheek, a small touch, but one of consolation. "Some stories are real. And a lot of stories that aren't real are still true."

"How is any of it true if it isn't real?"

His voice turned as soft as the hum of the heater.

"Robin Hood might not have existed. Maybe there was never a band of Merry Men waiting in Sherwood Forest for King Richard's return. But I'd like to think it happened. We've seen him in other times and places. Some people still stand up for what's right, some people do protect the helpless, some people fight for justice—and that's what makes the story of Robin Hood true."

Not real but true. I liked the thought.

I shut my eyes again, conjuring up the image of Robin Hood I'd had before. In my mind I reached out for him, saw myself with him, the mythic Robin Hood, and then I fell asleep.

I dreamt I walked with Robin Hood in the bright, sunlit forest. But my dreams never stay bright anymore. Eventually the forest turned dark, foreboding, and I walked alone. Even the birds stopped chirping, and I knew the Grim Reaper was there, gliding somewhere among the trees, sweeping all life into his cloak. He would find me soon.

Then I heard voices around me—Steve and someone else, and I remembered I was in the car, but felt too sleepy to move.

A voice that sounded like Steve but wasn't him said, "I see you have a new girl. What happened to the old one?"

"Which old one?" Steve asked.

"I don't suppose it really matters, does it?"

Now I was all the way awake, but I still didn't move. I didn't want them to know I'd heard them talking about me.

Steve said, "I broke up with Karli a couple of months ago."

"I guess I'm not up on my tabloid news. I thought you had something going on with the Maid Marion chick."

"That's just publicity hype." I felt Steve leaning over me, gently shaking me. "Annika, my brother is here. It's time to go."

I opened my eyes and blinked from the glare of the overhead light. The door stood open, and cold air billowed into the car. When my eyes adjusted, I saw him. His hair was lighter and he was a couple inches shorter than Steve, but the resemblance was still solid. He had the same jawline and soft brown eyes. He even had the same grin.

Steve helped me out of the car. I caught a glimpse of myself in the rearview mirror as he did. My hair looked thick and wild, like I'd emerged from the jungle.

"This is my brother, Adam. He's going to let us use his car."

"Hi," I said, my voice still heavy with sleep.

Adam walked over to his car, a red sporty-looking thing, which I couldn't identify and was too tired to care about. He shook his head. "You can borrow my car, but not until you come home and spend the night at Mom and Dad's."

"That wasn't our agreement," Steve said.

"It's too dangerous to drive through the night." Adam opened his car door and slid in behind the wheel. "You'll fall asleep at the wheel."

"It's only ten-fifteen," Steve said tightly.

"But it will be a lot later when you're driving back to California. Do you want to use my car or not?"

Steve took a step toward his brother. "I paid for this car, you know."

"Yeah, and you put the title in my name." Adam shut the car door, but leaned out the window. "What? You think a good night's rest will kill you?"

Steve folded his arms. "Mom and Dad do not want me to spend the night."

"Yes, they do. Besides, it will be eleven by the time we get home, so chances are they'll be asleep."

I knew Adam was lying. Probably Steve did too. I said, "We've got to drive to Henderson now. Steve's got to be back at the studio in the morning."

Steve glanced at his watch with resignation. "Jeremy is asleep. And even if we did drive straight there, you wouldn't want me to wake him up at midnight to teach him how to shoot a bow and arrow. We'll get a few hours of sleep and go early in the morning. I'll call the studio and ask them if they can shoot my scenes in the afternoon."

Steve took another step toward the car, but I didn't move. Technically his eleven-hour obligation to me would be over by then. I hoped that wouldn't make a difference to him. He turned back and took my hand. "Come on, Annika, you're shivering." I let him pull me into the car and phoned my parents to tell them what had happened.

They weren't happy about this new turn of events. My dad kept saying that he was going to drive down and pick me up, and I kept pointing out that I'd be safer at Steve's parents' house than sitting out on the freeway for the next hour and a half waiting for him.

"You want me to let you go off to a stranger's house?" Dad said.

Which upset me on Steve's behalf. He was after all spending a lot of time and effort to visit Jeremy, who was a stranger to him. But I couldn't say any of that with Steve sitting in the car in front of me. "Steve's a good guy," I whispered into the phone. "This is really one of those judgment things you're going to have to trust me on."

There was a long pause and then Dad said, "There's only one reason I'm not in the car already: I do trust your judgment." Another pause. "But I still want you to call me when you get to the Raleighs' house."

That made me smile. "I will. And I'll be home first thing in the morning."

"You'd better be. It's our day to spend with Jeremy."

He didn't need to remind me about that. We were all taking off from school and work to spend the last day before surgery with Jeremy. "I'll be there," I told him, "and I'll bring him his special surprise."

The trip to the Raleighs' house was uneventful. I sat in the car wishing we weren't backtracking on I-15. Steve and Adam talked, getting caught up with one another, but in a stiff manner. I didn't quite know what to make of Adam. He seemed to both resent and admire his brother, and I didn't know how such contradictory emotions could fit together.

Finally, as the clock crept toward eleven, we pulled up to a large stucco and stone house flanked on either side by spindly Palo Verdes. The porch light shone dimly against the front door, dwarfed by the interior lights. Adam pulled into the four-car garage, got out, and retrieved Steve's bag. "Looks like someone is up, after all." Adam tried to feign surprise but didn't really do a good job of it. I knew he'd brought us here because he wanted Steve and his parents to meet. Adam swung Steve's bag over his shoulder and walked inside without giving either of us a backward glance.

Steve and I dragged ourselves out of the car. He put

his hand on my back, guiding me to the door, but he did it so tensely I wondered whether he was using me as a shield.

We walked through a laundry room and into a sprawling kitchen. A stone floor spread out before us. Nothing cluttered up the black marble countertops—a kitchen clearly not frequented by six-year-olds. I took it all in for a moment, then turned to Steve's parents. They sat at an elegant table waiting for us.

I don't know what I had expected. Perhaps people who looked glamorous enough to give birth to a TV star. They looked like regular parents, though. Mr. Raleigh was tall and still fairly fit, with a receding hairline. He smiled at us, but his wrinkles gave him a stern expression. Mrs. Raleigh had blond hair that still looked perfectly coiffed this late at night, and she wore traces of makeup. Only the extra weight she carried saved her from looking immaculate. It softened her and made her look huggable. Steve just nodded in their direction, though. "Mom. Dad."

His mother stood and walked toward us, her glance switching back and forth between Steve and me. She seemed not to know what to do with her hands. "Hello, Steven." Her glance settled on me. "Are you going to introduce us to your friend?"

Even though I could sense the tension in his body, Steve's voice came out casual. "This is Annika Truman.

We were driving to her home in Nevada when we ran into car problems. . . ."

His gaze turned to his brother, who leaned up against the kitchen counter. "I called Adam, and he insisted we come here for the night."

Mrs. Raleigh forced a smile. "Oh, you're meeting her parents. It must be serious, then." She examined me more thoroughly. "Well, it's nice we get to meet her too, even if it only was because your car broke down—"

"It's not like that," Steve said.

I quickly added, "He's not going to my house to meet my parents. He's going to meet my little brother. Jeremy is a big fan of the show, and he's having surgery on Friday. Steve agreed to come and talk to him for a while."

"Oh." Her tone was so gentle you almost missed the edge to it. "You're going to go spend time with Annika's brother. How nice." She cast a glance back in Adam's direction, I presume to see if he felt slighted by this snub.

"My brother is six years old," I said. It felt as though I was inserting random facts into the conversation, but I wanted to make it clear he couldn't possibly be Adam's rival.

Then no one said anything. I could nearly taste the tension in the room. Mr. Raleigh sat silently at the table, one hand clenched, watching his son. Adam split his gazes between his father and his brother, looking at them with equal parts hope and reproach. He wanted something to happen; I didn't know what. Steve's mom didn't watch him at all—she kept examining me. She hadn't decided whether to like or resent me.

I couldn't see Steve's facial expression because he stood behind me, but I silently cursed him for not giving me any warning as to what I should say and how I should act. I'd expected him to tell his parents we'd just met, but he didn't offer any further details about me. In fact, he didn't say anything else.

Apparently I was the only one here who wasn't somehow emotionally charged, which meant I should be the one to speak next. "Thank you for letting us stay here," I said. "We appreciate it."

"You're welcome," Mrs. Raleigh said. "Our home is always open to you." She smiled as she said it, but I could tell her words were an accusation, not an invitation. She was hurt he hadn't come of his own free will. "So how long have the two of you been dating?"

Steve said, "Not long," then put his hand on my back again. "Look, it's late and Annika is tired. Why don't you give her the guest room, and I'll sleep on the couch."

Mr. Raleigh finally spoke. "We haven't seen you for three years and you want to rush off to bed?"

Steve let out a slow breath. "You have to work in the morning. I figured you'd rather sleep, but if you want to talk—fine. What did you want to talk about?"

Mrs. Raleigh took a step toward her husband. "We're all tired. We'll feel better after a good night's sleep." She turned back to me. "I'll show you the bathroom, and you can change into your pajamas."

"Actually, I don't have any."

Mrs. Raleigh's eyebrows shot up, so I added, "We planned on reaching my house before nighttime. I have clothes there."

"Oh." Mrs. Raleigh let out a relieved breath. "I have a nightgown you can borrow, then. Why don't you give me your clothes and I'll wash them so they'll be clean for tomorrow." She ran a critical eye over my outfit, and her gaze stopped on Steve's shirt. She stared at it, puzzled, and I wondered if she recognized it.

"Actually, these aren't my clothes. I just borrowed them from Steve." Which was the wrong thing to say to a guy's mother. Her eyebrows shot back up. "But only because I was a nun. And . . . and I couldn't really go home in a nun's habit—"

Mrs. Raleigh's eyebrows stayed up. "I suppose not."

Adam looked at Steve in astonishment. "You're corrupting nuns?"

"She's not a real nun," Steve said. "She played one on the show."

"We left for Nevada really suddenly," I added, "and the costume department had sent my clothes out to be cleaned."

"You're an actress, then?" Mrs. Raleigh asked.

"No, not really. Well, sort of. I was a temporary extra." At this point, I figured it would not reassure her if I said I was a high school student who had snuck on the set to stalk her son, so I didn't volunteer that information.

She didn't press the point. Instead she smiled and motioned me to follow her. "I'll get you something to wear now. We'll have time in the morning to talk. Then you can tell me how you and Steve met."

I followed her out of the kitchen but flung a worried look back at Steve. I was not about to tell his mother how we met, and I didn't want him to, either.

Steve shrugged and grinned at me, which was not encouraging.

I trailed Mrs. Raleigh through the house and stood in the doorway of her bedroom while she sifted through a dresser drawer murmuring, "Not that one . . . you'd freeze in that. . . ."

As Mrs. Raleigh rifled through her nightgowns, I looked at the things on her dresser: a golden-framed picture of Adam, a flower arrangement, a jeweled bowl, and ornate candleholders. At my house, the only candles we own are shoved in a drawer in case the electricity goes out.

Finally Mrs. Raleigh found a nightgown she deemed suitable. She took a folded flannel garment from her drawer and walked it over to me. "This will be perfect for you. Grandma Nora made it for me years ago, but I've never worn it."

And as soon as I unfolded it, the reason became clear. Not only was it made with industrial-strength flannel—I mean, honestly, it could have been used to line sleeping bags—lacy ruffles ran up and down the front. Ruffles also ringed the high collar and the sleeves. It looked like something a pioneer schoolmarm would wear.

Next, Mrs. Raleigh found a toothbrush for me, showed me to the bathroom, and then waited out in the hallway for me to change so she could wash my clothes. "I can find something from my wardrobe for you to wear tomorrow if you'd rather," she said.

I handed her the pile of clothes. "That's okay. Steve's stuff is fine." After seeing her choice of nightgown, I was not about to trust her to pick out clothes for me.

I crawled into the bed in the guest room and tried to sleep, but my mind kept replaying the scene in the kitchen, reexamining the conversation. I thought about how sad it would be if I came home and didn't feel welcome.

I heard voices coming from the master bedroom. Even hushed, I could pick out the notes of harshness in the conversation. Steve's parents weren't happy. Had seeing Steve upset them, or were they just hurt he hadn't greeted them more warmly?

The voices from Adam's room came in louder. He and Steve talked more naturally than they had in the car, perhaps because I wasn't there. Every once in a while I heard Adam's voice, pleading, but I couldn't make out what he said, except once. Steve said, as though making a point, "I didn't see any recent pictures of *me* hanging on the walls."

"They don't have to hang pictures of you on the walls," Adam said. "You're on reruns every night of the week. They never miss your show."

Then the voices softened back into unrecognizable murmurs.

It's hard to relax when you're in the middle of someone else's tension. And it's even harder to sleep when you know the Grim Reaper might be waiting for you at the edge of consciousness.

I thought of my story for Jeremy and tried to come up with an ending he would like. How did one get out of the underworld? How did one outsmart death? I wandered around in my imagination, traveling to the cavernous gulf of the afterlife. I felt the walls, looking for cracks. I only had my bow and arrows, a flock of crows—which may or may not prove useful—and my wits. With this small arsenal, I had to figure out a way to bring Jeremy back home with me.

It was like one of those riddles you can't quite bend your mind around to find the answer. Or maybe an answer didn't exist at all. If death could be tricked, surely someone smarter than me would have figured out the way by now.

Then a worse thought came to me: How did anything we ever did in life matter when we all ended up dead anyway?

I would never fall asleep at this rate. I pulled myself out of bed. I might as well get a drink of water to clear my mind and try again.

The voices had stopped from both rooms, so I hadn't expected to run into anyone in the hallway, but Steve emerged from the bathroom as I walked up.

He looked me up and down. "I see my mother tried to make you feel comfortable by providing you with a nun-approved nightgown."

He turned to walk around me, so I stepped in front of him and lowered my voice. "I don't know what I'm supposed to say to your family in the morning. In fact, I don't know what I'm supposed to say at all."

His voice dropped to a whisper. "We'll leave early, and there won't be time for a lot of conversation. I'll get you up at five-thirty, okay?"

I should have felt relieved, but I didn't. I only thought of the way Mrs. Raleigh's eyes had reflected pain when she'd said "Our home is always open to you."

"Your parents want to talk to you and you're going to leave before they have a chance?"

"We need to make it to your house at a decent hour. It's a two-and-a-half-hour drive."

He made as if to go around me, and I shifted my position so he couldn't. "Why don't you want to talk to them?"

He faced me, his expression suddenly weary, and he rubbed the back of his neck. "What do you already know? What did the internet say?"

"You petitioned the courts when you were sixteen to be made an adult because you didn't want your parents spending your money."

He let out a sigh, looked down the hallway toward his parents' bedroom, then pulled me into the bathroom. Even after the door shut, he kept his voice low. "It wasn't that I didn't want them spending my money, it was just that—" He let out another sigh. "Do you remember how I told you I made a lot of money as a child?"

I nodded.

"I made over three million dollars by the time I reached sixteen, but my parents had spent almost all of it. They kept buying nicer houses, nicer cars. I said I wanted to invest it—so then they bought jewelry and artwork—which might have worked, if either of them had known anything about jewelry or artwork. They didn't, though. They just liked living like millionaires.

"Child actors tend to have short careers. Robin Hood is popular now, but fads pass quickly, and there's a good chance I'll be a has-been by age twenty-one. When I landed the part of Robin Hood, I tried talking to them about managing my finances, but that didn't change anything. So I talked to the show's lawyers."

He shook his head and grimaced. "If you ever want to take a bad situation and make it horrible, just add a couple of lawyers. I only wanted some control over how my money was being spent, but my parents didn't see it like that. My dad told me if I felt that way, I could get out of his house and live on my own." Steve leaned back against the counter and looked past me into nothing. "So I did. And they moved here, and we haven't talked to each other since."

"Have you tried to talk to them?"

He sent me a look to show me that I had clearly missed the point of his story.

I said, "So now you have your money, but you've lost your family?"

He straightened, reminding me with that simple movement how tall he was. "You think I should have let my parents spend it all?"

"No, but shouldn't you try to mend fences? Don't you still love them?"

He set his jaw. "It was never about not loving them,

but after the lawyers got involved, my parents treated me like a stranger." He held out his hand to me as though offering proof. "In the five minutes I just spent with them, my dad couldn't say anything nice, my mother slid in one accusation after another, and my brother thinks I'm out corrupting nuns." The corners of his mouth tilted up as he said this—as though he couldn't maintain his anger in the face of such a suggestion.

I stared back at him. I'd done nothing for the last month but worry about my own family falling apart, and he and his parents had walked away from each other. It seemed like such a waste. "So you retaliate by refusing to let them have any part in your life."

"That isn't true."

"You don't tell them what's going on with you at all, do you?"

"I don't have to. That's what *People* magazine is for."

I put one hand on my hip, immediately engulfing it in flannel. "You wouldn't even tell them the truth about us."

He shrugged. "They asked how long we'd dated. What did you want me to do—check my watch and say, 'About six and a half hours'?"

I sent him a disbelieving look. "You consider this a date?"

He leaned back on the counter with his arms folded and didn't concede the point. "I bought you dinner. I kissed you."

"It was yogurt and a muffin from a gas station, and you were pretending I was Maid Marion when you kissed me."

"I kissed you before that."

"No, *I* kissed *you* before that."

He let out an exasperated grunt and closed the distance between us. "Okay, fine. Does this count?"

Before I realized what he was doing he put his hands on my shoulders, bent down, and kissed me. Some people will do anything to win an argument. I shouldn't have let him. I should have pushed him away and accused him of trying to corrupt nuns again. But I didn't. I wound my arms around his neck, kissed him back, and felt my heartbeat double.

He finally lifted his head and smiled down at me.

"Okay," I said. "That counts, but it still doesn't change the fact that you're not trying to work things out with your family."

He let out a groan and stepped away from me.

I watched him distance himself from me. "I would pay any amount of money to still have a relationship with my brother when he's seventeen. You can have that if you want. Think about what you're losing."

We regarded each other in silence for a moment. His

eyes remained hard. I hadn't changed his mind. He ran a hand across his hair. "Look, it's late. We both need our sleep."

As he walked past me, I said, "After we go to Henderson, will we ever see each other again?"

He paused in the doorway. "I'd like to."

"I'd like to too." I smiled at him, even though his statement was less than decisive.

He said good night, and we went our separate ways. The phrase "I'd like to" echoed through my mind all the way back to my room.

I'd like to. And I'd also like to travel around the world. I'd like to win a gold medal in archery. I'd like to fly. I'd like to save my brother's life.

He was a huge star who could have his pick of Hollywood starlets, and I was a nobody from Nevada. No, I was worse than a nobody; I was broken glass. Why would he choose me when there were women like Esme and Karli fighting for him? I doubted I'd ever see him again after tomorrow.

Chapter 15

It took me a while to get to sleep, but if I dreamt of the Grim Reaper, I didn't remember it. The next thing I knew, Mrs. Raleigh opened the bedroom door. She put my stack of clothes on the dresser, and I blinked at the muted light coming through a crack in the curtains. "What time is it?"

"Almost seven. I thought you'd want your clothes when you woke up."

"Seven?" I got out of bed so fast I momentarily went dizzy. I tried to do the math. If we were two and a half hours away from Henderson, and then he spent half an hour with Jeremy—he wasn't going to make it to work until two o'clock. He'd have to speed both ways. "Where is Steve?" I asked. "Is he ready to go?"

"Oh, no, he just got out of the shower. He hasn't even had breakfast yet. I'm making pancakes and eggs."

"That's really nice of you, but Steve wanted to leave early—" I grabbed the clothes from the dresser. I needed to change, and I couldn't do that with her standing in the room.

She walked to the curtains and opened them all the way. "I think he's worked things out with the studio. He called them this morning." There was a lightness in her step that hadn't been there last night, and her voice sounded happy. "He said a big breakfast would be fine. It will be done by the time you get out of the shower."

I took a fast shower and hurried getting ready anyway. It was odd to see my hair brown in the mirror, as though even my reflection wasn't sure who I was.

When I walked into the kitchen, the entire family sat around the table eating. It seemed so tranquil. If I hadn't been part of the kitchen scene last night, I wouldn't have known they didn't get along.

Mrs. Raleigh held out a pitcher of orange juice to Steve. "Would you like more?"

He spread a dab of butter onto his pancake. "No, thanks. I'm fine."

An empty seat waited for me, but I didn't take it. Instead I caught Steve's eye. "We have time to eat?"

He motioned to the chair. "It's all right. Sit down and have breakfast."

"Yeah," Adam added, "you're not getting out of telling us how you met Steve."

"Steve wouldn't tell us," Mrs. Raleigh clarified with a teasing smile that reminded me of her son's. "He said we'd have to hear the story from you."

I sat down. "Did he?"

Mrs. Raleigh handed me the pancake plate, and I took one. I was glad Steve was talking to his parents but less thrilled by his choice of topics. I poured myself a glass of orange juice.

"So did you meet on the *Robin Hood* series?" Mr. Raleigh asked.

I glanced at Steve. He took a bite of his eggs so he wouldn't have to speak. Since I probably was never going to see these people again, I decided I could improve on the truth. "Actually, no. We met at an archery contest. I beat Steve, by the way."

"You beat Robin Hood?" Adam laughed as he cut through a pancake. "Is that possible? My faith in the show has been completely destroyed."

"It was his overconfidence that cost him the match," I said.

"No," Steve said, "I think it had something to do with your being president of your archery club. She didn't let me know about that beforehand."

I smiled at Adam. "You can see it's a sore subject with us."

"One of these days we'll have to have a rematch," Steve said.

I laughed and ate my pancake. Then I took another. The breakfast went on in the same light tone, with Steve and his family making small talk about the show and old family friends.

I thought the subject of my relationship with Steve had completely passed, but out of the blue, Mrs. Raleigh said, "I'm surprised I haven't seen anything about you and Annika in the tabloids."

"Well, that won't last," Steve said. "They caught us yesterday and followed us halfway here. That's how we damaged the car. We went over a median to lose them."

Adam leaned back in his chair. "It's nice to see your driving hasn't changed over the years."

Steve glanced at me but didn't correct his brother.

I said, "I hope we don't run into paparazzi today. I'm wearing the same clothes. They'll either think I have a very limited fashion sense or you've taken up with a homeless girl."

Steve didn't even crack a smile. He looked down and turned the fork in his hand slowly. "About today," he said, returning his gaze to my face. "I called Dean's assistant and told him I wouldn't be in until the afternoon, but Dean called me back himself and told me they needed me in this morning. I have to leave for Burbank as soon as the rental car company drops off a car." He glanced at his watch. "Which should be any minute now."

My mouth opened to protest, but he went on. "I've talked to Adam about it, and he can drive you to Henderson today. Ron will book me on a flight to Las Vegas tomorrow night. I'll come to the hospital as soon as we complete shooting for the day."

It hurt to swallow. The words felt ragged as they came from my throat. "I already told my family I was bringing you with me."

"I know. Unfortunately, the studio needs me."

"My brother needs you more."

His voice was thick with resignation. "I'm sorry. I tried, but it didn't work out. I'll be there tomorrow night."

My fork shook in my hand, and I had to put it back down on the table. I could feel the weight of everyone's stares on me. The clank of silverware at the table had gone completely silent.

I tried not to panic, or at least not to show that I was. "Jeremy has to see you before the surgery. He needs to believe that his wishes have power so he won't be afraid, so it will go well. I explained it to you—"

Steve leaned toward me. "Annika, my visit isn't going to make a difference in the outcome of the surgery."

He might as well have said he didn't care. It felt as though all the air had gone from my lungs. "Don't say that. It isn't true."

His tone came out smooth, painless. "I can't hold

up the entire production schedule. I'm under contract."

I wanted to say, "How can you do this to me?" but it was a stupid question. I'd only known him a day. What had I expected? And what had happened to me, anyway, that after one day I felt the two of us knew each other intimately? I would have moved heaven and earth to fulfill Jeremy's wish. Steve wouldn't even skip a day of work.

Steve's family had all gone back to their breakfasts, pointedly pretending that it wasn't awkward to hear all of this.

"Tell Jeremy I'll be there tomorrow night," Steve said. "He'll understand."

Jeremy might, but I refused to understand. My voice came out as a whisper. "What if tomorrow night is too late?"

The doorbell rang. Steve glanced in that direction and then back at me. "It won't be." He pushed his chair away from the table. "That's got to be the car."

Everyone watched him. The warmth, all the feelings of coziness had drained from the room.

Steve stood up but turned to his father. "I'll have Ron wire some money for the towing charge. Let me know how much it comes to."

An edge crept into his father's voice. "You don't have to. We can cover it."

"You shouldn't have to cover it. It's not your car."

"You don't need to pay us anything. We don't need your money."

Steve's eyes narrowed. "You're being ridiculous."

"Am I?"

Mrs. Raleigh put her hand to her mouth, but didn't say anything. Adam looked up at the ceiling.

"Fine," Steve said tightly. "Do whatever you want. It was great to see all of you again." He turned and strode toward the kitchen door.

Mr. Raleigh said to me—although clearly for Steve's benefit, "It's always been this way. His job takes precedence over everybody else."

Steve stiffened and muttered something under his breath, but he didn't turn around. After a moment, the front door slammed shut.

I turned my attention back to the table and felt numb. Steve was right to have given me the news after breakfast. Otherwise I wouldn't have been able to eat.

No one spoke. I felt them watching me, pitying me. I struggled to find my voice, and I looked over at Adam. "When do you want to leave?"

"Give me a few minutes. I've got to call someone about getting assignments."

I was making him miss school. It made me feel even worse.

Mrs. Raleigh stood up and cleared dishes from the

table. I helped her, trying to be polite, trying to do something so I didn't have to think about what to say to Jeremy when I got home.

The genie ran into a problem with Robin Hood. Would Jeremy ever believe me about anything again?

If I had been thinking straight, I would have made Steve talk to him on the cell phone beforehand, but maybe Jeremy wouldn't have liked that. Robin Hood never used a cell phone on the show.

As I helped her with the dishes, Mrs. Raleigh threw worried glances in my direction. "I'm sorry it's been a difficult trip for you," she told me. "I hope things go well for your brother."

"Thanks. And thanks again for letting me stay here."

"Maybe you'll come back sometime."

I hesitated. "Maybe."

She read her own meaning into my hesitation. "It hasn't always been this way between Steve and his father. They used to get along so well. I keep hoping . . ." She rinsed off a plate and slid it into the dishwasher. "Maybe you could talk with him about it. Sometimes a woman's influence can—"

I didn't let her finish. I couldn't explain to her why I had no influence on Steve and why any conversation I had with him after today would be very limited.

"I have talked with him about it," I said. It was, after

all, the truth. We'd talked in the bathroom last night. "I already told him he should work on his relationship with you."

"Really?" Mrs. Raleigh asked. The gratitude in her voice made me feel guilty. "What did he say?"

"Well. . . ." I couldn't tell her that he'd brushed off my words, not while she looked at me so hopefully. "He's stubborn—you know that—but he's also said some nice things about you." As I spoke, Adam and Mr. Raleigh walked into the kitchen. Their conversation died as they listened to mine.

I struggled to think of anything nice Steve had said about them. When that failed, I decided elaborations were in order. After all, I didn't owe Steve any honesty. He'd run off and left me with his disgruntled family.

I looked over at Mr. Raleigh. "He told me about how you were a police officer and how worried he was when you got stabbed. He said when he works on Robin Hood and he needs to portray bravery, he thinks of you."

Mr. Raleigh stared back at me, stunned, and didn't speak. To Mrs. Raleigh I said, "Steve told me about all the sacrifices you've made for him over the years and how he never would have succeeded if you hadn't been there hauling him to all those auditions."

Instead of putting her juice glass into the dishwasher, Mrs. Raleigh stopped halfway, then simply held on to it.

I turned to Adam. "Steve misses you. He wishes the two of you were closer."

It wasn't real, but it was true anyway, so Steve couldn't get mad at me for saying any of it.

The ride to Henderson took a long time—mostly because Adam never inched a mile above the speed limit. I didn't know other people besides Madison actually drove this way. Apparently I'd found her soul mate. The ride wasn't nearly as awkward as I anticipated, though. I mean, I didn't know Adam. I'd barely spoken to him at all, but somehow my conversation in the kitchen had transformed me into his confidant. We'd barely pulled out of the driveway before he gave me his side of the story.

"I want to be close to Steve too, but he's put me in the middle of everything. How am I supposed to get along with my parents and also be on Steve's side?" Adam kept his eyes on the road, but I knew his concentration wasn't there. "Besides, I'm not sure I agree with what Steve did. After all, for years our parents supported Steve—Dad was out on the street dodging bullets to put food on the table—Steve owes him some gratitude for that." A hard edge crept into his voice. "Can't he understand how it made Dad feel when Steve not only became more financially successful, but then cut his parents off?"

I kicked myself for even caring about all of this. If I

ever saw Steve again, it would probably only be for a few minutes, and yet I still sat there in the car trying to solve his problems. I listened to Adam, agreeing, reassuring, suggesting, and in general trying to find ways to smooth things out between them.

The strange thing was that as I talked to Adam, I found a part of me loosening, coming alive again, as though ungripping my fist after holding it tightly for a long time. Things could be worse at my house, I realized. There were a lot of ways to lose a brother.

But as we pulled into Henderson, all my anxiety about facing my parents and disappointing Jeremy returned—and then some. We'd talked so much about Steve's relationship with his family that we'd barely talked about me. However, one thing became clear: Adam thought I lived in California and was going back home to visit my brother.

I'd let Adam believe this because it seemed way easier than explaining the last two days. Steve had already told them we were dating—and besides, the Raleighs had been so eager to meet me and so touched by the things I'd told them. How could I yank that away from them now and tell them I barely knew Steve?

As we drove down the familiar streets to my house, it occurred to me I'd have to invite Adam inside. And once he met my parents, he was bound to say something that didn't make sense to them, like, "It was nice to spend time with Annika. We don't usually meet Steve's girl-friends."

This would call for all sorts of awkward explanations where I would either look like a girlfriend impostor or like I'd been carrying on some clandestine relationship with a guy in another state behind my parents' backs.

We pulled into my neighborhood. I drummed my fingers against the armrest as I tried to think of a way around this.

"What's wrong?" Adam asked. "It sounds like you're trying to send a telegraph through the car door."

I stopped my tapping. "Sorry. I was just thinking about our dogs. They get excited when new people come to the house."

He smiled as though he liked dogs. "What kind are they?"

"We have two pit bulls," I lied. "Dagger and Death-wish, but don't worry; Mom and Dad usually muzzle them when they know someone is coming. They sort of have to now. Police orders." I pointed to an upcoming street. "Turn left on Brooksfarm."

He turned left. "Police orders?"

"Yeah . . . your dogs chase one salesman up a tree, and the police get all over your case."

"Oh," he said.

"It's not like it was that big of a deal. I mean, okay, the dogs probably shouldn't have eaten the guy's shoes, especially while he was wearing them, but it's not like they were expensive." I shrugged casually. "Besides, if you can't climb fast enough, those sorts of things are bound to happen to you."

Adam didn't say anything, but I noticed his grip tighten on the steering wheel.

"It's not like people don't have extra toes," I said.

His posture stiffened.

"My house is right there," I said. "The one with the big claw marks on the front door."

He pulled into my driveway, but didn't turn off the car. He looked over at me without letting go of the steering wheel. "It was really nice to meet you, Annika. I'm glad we had time to talk on the drive."

"It was great to get to know you too." I opened my door.

He fingered the steering wheel. "I would see you inside, but, uh, I've got to hurry and get back."

I slid out of the car. "All right, next time, then. Thanks again for the ride."

I watched him drive away and then walked slowly to my house. I'd only been gone a couple days, but it seemed like so much longer. Everything looked different, subtly changed somehow. I opened the front door and called out, "I'm home."

I expected Jeremy to be the first one to greet me, but

Mom and Leah walked into the front room. Mom actually stopped in her tracks when she saw me. "Good heavens, what have you done to your hair?"

I'd forgotten about it, and I fingered the ends of my hair. "Oh, that. I dyed it so Steve Raleigh wouldn't recognize me."

Leah tilted her head at me questioningly. "And why would Steve Raleigh recognize you?"

Mom looked over my shoulder and around the room. "Where is he?"

"He got called back to the studio this morning. His brother, Adam, dropped me off."

"He got called back to the studio?" Leah repeated.

"His brother didn't come inside with you?" Mom asked. I could tell neither one of them believed me, which just proves karma exists, after all. I'd lied to the Raleighs and not been caught, so it figured that now when I told the truth, my own family wouldn't believe me.

"Look, didn't you talk to Madison? Didn't she tell you how I met Steve Raleigh on the set?"

Leah and Mom exchanged a glance that I couldn't interpret. The disbelief didn't leave their faces.

"Okay," I said, "Madison didn't actually see me meet him on the set because she got kicked off for hauling a snake around, only she didn't really do that. But I did. I mean, I did meet Steve Raleigh. And we had an archery match, and I won, so he had to come home with me. Only he got called back to the studio this morning and so he said he'd come tomorrow night, and I think he will, but I'm not sure because, hey, he said he'd come this time and he didn't."

My mother and sister stared at me silently, so I added, "See, I'm wearing his clothes. That proves it."

"Really?" Leah said without emotion. "Did he write his name in them or something?"

I ignored her. "I'm not sure if I should tell Jeremy about Steve's visit tomorrow. I want to tell him because then he'll have something to look forward to, but I don't want to disappoint him again. I think Steve will come because he's a nice guy, and after all, he did tell his parents we were dating. You don't do that and then not show up at a girl's house. So maybe I should tell Jeremy. What do you think?"

Leah said, "I think you've lost your mind."

Mom, in a gentle voice, said, "Honey, I don't think you should tell Jeremy anything right now."

"I'm telling you the truth," I said. "The paparazzi even got pictures of us together."

Leah let out a slow breath and shook her head. "This is so sad."

I couldn't argue the fact any further because Dad and Jeremy walked in the room.

"Look who's home," Mom said cheerfully, but both of them just stared at me speechlessly.

I knelt down and opened my arms to give Jeremy a hug. Instead of running to my arms, he walked up and touched my hair gingerly.

"What happened to your hair?"

"I dyed it."

"It died?" Before I could explain, he added, "You mean when you cut it off in the underworld?"

"The underworld?" Leah asked. "Did you go there before or after you went to Hollywood?"

To Jeremy I said, "That was a story. It was just pretend."

"But the underworld is real, though," he said.

I didn't know how to answer. Before I could think of what to say, he stroked my hair and said, "I bet the crows gave you new hair, didn't they, because they wanted you to look pretty. When will you finish that story?"

I pulled him into a hug so I wouldn't have to look at his face. His body felt so small against mine. I trembled and didn't know how to stop. "I'll finish it later. Don't worry; I won't leave us in the underworld, but I just got home. I need to change clothes."

He pushed away from me. "Mom and Dad said you brought me a surprise. What is it?"

I didn't say anything, but his gaze held me, expecting

an answer. It physically hurt to speak. "The surprise didn't work out like I'd expected. I'll have to give it to you later."

Out of the corner of my eye, I could see Mom shaking her head. She didn't want me to say any more about it.

Jeremy leaned toward me. "Is it about the genie?"

I put my finger to his lips. "Shhh. You weren't supposed to tell about that."

The doorbell rang. I could tell by my parents' expressions they weren't expecting anyone. Right then, a sinking feeling came over me. I knew it was Adam. I must have left something in the car, or maybe he'd had some sort of car problems. In a moment I'd have to introduce him to everyone as Steve's brother.

It wouldn't help the case for my story or my sanity when he walked nervously into the room mumbling, "Don't let Dagger and Deathwish get me!"

My father went to the door. I bit my lip and wondered how I always got myself into these predicaments. Right then I swore I would never lie again. From now on karma would have no reason to bite me.

My father opened the door, and Steve walked in.

Chapter 16

Steve wore the Robin Hood costume, right down to the bow in his hands and the boots on his feet. I must admit he made an impressive figure, decked out in Lincoln green in our doorway. For several seconds, I found it hard to breathe.

Steve turned as though addressing someone in our driveway, waved, and in a perfect English accent said, "Thanks, Genie, it looks like this is the right house."

Jeremy ran over to him. "You're Robin Hood!"

Steve laughed and said, "I am. And you must be the tyke that needs archery lessons."

"My name is Jeremy," he said.

Steve bent down to be on Jeremy's level. "When do you want to start? We've got some work cut out for us if we're to get you to the point where you can beat Annika."

"No one can beat Annika," Jeremy said, and then

thought better of it. "Except for you. You're the best archer in the whole world."

Steve glanced in my direction and smiled. "Well, some people might argue otherwise."

At this point, I remembered my manners and introduced Robin Hood to my family. Leah, I swear, nearly swooned. While Steve shook my parents' hands, she grabbed hold of my arm and whispered, "I've got to get my camera. And all my friends."

"Don't you dare call your friends," I told her. "This is Jeremy's time."

She let out a whimper, but didn't contradict me.

Jeremy took Steve by the hand, and jumping up and down with excitement, turned to my dad. "Can we get the target out now? Can we?"

So my dad hauled it out of the garage and into the backyard, and Jeremy ran to his room to retrieve his bow and arrows. After he left, Mom put her hand against her chest and said, "I really can't thank you enough for this, Mr. Raleigh."

"Call me Robin," he said. "Today I'm only Robin."

"Robin," she repeated with a smile.

I took a step toward him and lowered my voice in case Jeremy came back. "I thought they needed you on the set?"

"I called Dean and told him I had an appointment I couldn't miss."

"What made you change your mind?"

He took a step toward me and whispered, "While I drove out of Apple Valley, I kept remembering how you said the real Robin Hood would come see Jeremy." He shrugged in an offhand manner, but his eyes were intense. "I've spent so much time playing him, for once I wanted to see what it felt like to really be him."

"How does it feel?" I asked.

He smiled back at me. "Good."

"How did you get here so quickly?"

He rubbed his jaw, reluctant to tell me. "On occasion I've been known to drive fast."

Jeremy ran back into the room with the bow gripped in his hand. "The target's ready!"

We all went outside. Steve and Jeremy stood near the target; the rest of us watched from a distance. I couldn't keep my eyes off of them. It was dreamlike: Robin Hood and my brother shooting arrows in our backyard.

Mom managed to take quite a bit of video and more pictures than we would ever need. She kept repeating, "This is so wonderful." She hugged me and said, "You did a good thing, Annika."

Even my father, who'd yelled at me for going to California, put his hand on my shoulder and said, "You made Jeremy very happy today. Just don't ever do anything like this again. Ever. I mean it."

Steve mostly ignored the rest of us and gave Jeremy

his full attention. Besides being a good actor, he was also a good teacher. Even after an hour, his enthusiasm didn't wear off. He bent down and put his arms around Jeremy, helping him aim the bow. "You've got it now. That's a good lad."

The arrow landed right outside the bull's-eye. Steve put his hand on Jeremy's shoulder. "That's the kind of shooting that worries King John. I hereby make you an honorary Merry Man."

Jeremy let out a happy gasp. "Really?"

Steve raised a hand. "I swear it by King Richard himself." He sized Jeremy up, then added, "We don't have any Lincoln greens in your size, but I dare say Maid Marion can make you some before long. I'll get them to you as soon as they're sewn."

Jeremy leaned around Steve and shouted to us—as though we hadn't just heard the conversation, "I get to be a Merry Man!" He turned back to Steve. "Do I get my own horse?"

Steve laughed and looked at us. "You'll have to discuss that with your mum."

"Perhaps the two of you would like to take a break and have something to eat," Mom called back, in a clear attempt to erase thoughts of horses from Jeremy's mind.

"Can we have a feast?" Jeremy asked. "Can we shoot a deer?"

"Well, we can order pizza," Mom said.

Jeremy put his hands on his hips. "Robin Hood doesn't eat pizza, Mom."

Steve laid a hand on Jeremy's shoulder. "Do you like pizza?"

Jeremy nodded.

"Then I shall be happy to try it."

They went to the living room. I went to my room and changed into a pair of jeans and a shirt; something a little more flattering than Steve's lucky poker T-shirt. I folded his clothes into a neat pile so I could give them back to him later.

When I joined my family in the living room, Jeremy was peppering Steve with questions about Sherwood Forest, the Sheriff of Nottingham, and the responsibilities of a Merry Man.

I kept staring at Steve, trying to see the person I'd seen this morning, the one with the short brown hair and casual conversation. It was hard to remember that person because his Robin Hood came through so vibrantly. I hadn't really appreciated this about him on the set, back when I'd watched him do silly things like sword fight with the air. But now his eyes glowed while he talked about the perils of the forest. I half believed him myself.

When the pizza arrived—just cheese pizza for Jeremy because Mom wouldn't let him eat the nitrates in pepperoni—we all sat at the kitchen table. Jeremy made a big deal of showing Steve how to eat it, and Steve smiled and followed his directions.

I tried not to constantly look at him, and struggled to find something else to rest my gaze on. But I kept looking back to Steve. Every once in a while he sent a smile in my direction, which completely robbed me of coherent thought. I had to keep telling myself to stop it. He was only here because he promised to see Jeremy. I probably wouldn't ever see him after today.

When we finished with the pizza, he nodded in my mother's direction. "Thank you for your hospitality, m'lady, but I fear my time here grows short. I dare not stay away from Sherwood for long, lest it be invaded by knaves and cutthroats—or, worse yet, lest Friar Tuck eat all the food."

My mom leaned toward him. "Thank you again for coming. This has meant so much to Jeremy."

The last part of her statement probably wasn't necessary because Jeremy threw himself into Steve's lap. They had a few more Merry Men words together and then Steve stood up and Dad pried Jeremy away.

Steve thanked my parents again for the strange delicacy of pizza, then looked at me. "Before I go I'd like to have a word alone with Lady Annika." He glanced down at Jeremy and winked. "We need to discuss genie business."

"Of course," Mom said. "Annika, why don't you show him to the door, and the rest of us will stay here and clean up the dishes."

"We have this neat thing called a dishwasher," Jeremy called to him. "Do you want to see it?"

"Perhaps next time."

Jeremy's face lit up with hope. "Will the genie let you come again?"

"Didn't I say I'd come back to give you your Lincoln greens? You shall have them soon, genie or no genie."

Jeremy raised his hands and jumped in triumph. "Yessss!"

I took Steve's hand and pulled him from the kitchen before Jeremy volunteered to show him how all the appliances worked.

As we walked, I said, "First of all, you're amazing. Really. I even know better, and I found myself believing in you."

"Thank you," he said using his regular voice.

"I don't remember the last time Jeremy was so thrilled. This whole thing will totally work. I just know he's going to fly through surgery tomorrow."

A flicker of doubt crossed Steve's eyes, but he squeezed my hand. "Good. I'm glad you're happy."

"Oh, and the second thing I need to tell you about. When your brother asks, tell him our pit bulls loved you."

"Your pit bulls?"

"Yeah, Dagger and Deathwish—and stop raising your eyebrow at me. I had to think of an excuse so he wouldn't come inside. I played your girlfriend all morning, and I couldn't really introduce him to my family since they know I don't live in California."

Steve shrugged. "We could be having one of those long-distance relationships."

"Could we?" I asked and then felt like I'd said too much. I'd put him on the spot. Before he could speak, I said, "I hope you don't get into too much trouble for messing up the production schedule."

"They'll manage." He tilted his head and gave me one of his famous smirks. "Although if the next few episodes have me swimming through freezing rivers or being repeatedly beaten by King John's men, well, you'll know Dean is still ticked off."

I smiled and tried to memorize how his hand felt in mine. I knew in another moment he'd pull it away from me and leave.

Instead of pulling his hand away, he took a step closer to me. "Look, Annika, we should probably talk about us." He said this in that hesitant voice guys use when they really don't want to discuss a subject but feel obligated.

I didn't want to hear his next words. I let go of his

hand and put my own in the back pockets of my jeans. "You don't have to say it. I understand." I looked out the living room window to the front lawn. His car was nowhere in sight. "Where did you park?"

"Down the street. If Jeremy was in your front yard, I didn't want him to see Robin Hood pulling up to his house in a Lexus. It ruins the whole medieval illusion."

I craned my neck to see farther down the street, but still didn't see the car.

"Yes," Steve said. "I did in fact walk past all of your neighbors' houses wearing green tights, a pointy feathered hat, and carrying a bow."

I giggled despite myself. "I'm sorry. Do you want me to drive you back to your car?"

"Are you kidding? I've seen how you drive."

I gave him a playful shove. "I think you'd be safe for a block."

He leaned closer to me, and his voice lost its teasing edge. "We could."

"We could what?"

"We could have a long-distance relationship."

The words surprised me so much I just stared back at him. "Oh."

He put his hands on my shoulders. "I know it's only been a couple of days, but you already know me better than Karli ever did. You care about people, and you're passionate about helping them. Besides, I feel like . . ." His voice drifted off as though he didn't know how to say it. "Like we've known each other all along. I've always felt that."

I took a step closer to him and smiled. "Right, I could tell by the way you brushed me off at the stadium."

He grinned, remembering. "Okay, maybe it wasn't an immediate connection. It was a little later . . . actually, it was when you jumped past me between trailers. I knew I was in trouble from then on. That was what I nearly confessed to you back in the car." He bent down to kiss me, but I heard footsteps and turned my head. Jeremy had come into the room. The timing made me jump. If he had walked in two seconds later, we would have had to explain to him why Robin Hood was cheating on Maid Marion.

Jeremy tilted his head at us. "What are you two doing?"

"Robin was about to tell me a secret," I said. "And you were supposed to stay in the kitchen."

"I wanted to see the genie before it took Robin Hood back to Sherwood Forest. I'm ready to make the last wish."

"Oh. Right." I ran a hand through my hair trying to get my mind away from Steve-nearly-kissed-me mode and back to genie mode. I looked behind Jeremy to see if Mom or Dad was about to come fetch him. "We'd probably better do that in the den."

"Okay." Jeremy took Steve's hand and pulled him toward the hallway. "The den is over here. Are you going to disappear into a puff of smoke?"

"No, he's not," I said. "And, remember, you have to keep your eyes closed or the genie won't come." I sent Steve an apologetic look as I led the way to the den. Once inside, I had Jeremy sit on the chair in front of the computer. Steve stood by the door, which I left partially open. To Steve I mouthed the words, "Once he shuts his eyes, leave."

Steve nodded.

"Remember," I told Jeremy, "for the official third wish you're going to wish that you do fine during surgery."

Jeremy shut his eyes, but then they popped open again. "You never told me what your first wish was."

"Well, it was a long time ago. . . ." I stalled. I still hadn't thought of a good answer to this question. What could I have wished for that he would believe? If only something amazing had happened in my past, something I could point to and say, "See, that was obviously the work of magic."

"Don't you remember what you wished for?" Jeremy asked.

"I remember . . . it's just private."

Jeremy lowered his voice. "I won't tell. Promise."

From beside the door Steve said, "I know what she wished for." I looked at him questioningly and he added, "I asked the genie. I had to know what kind of wish I followed. When you're part of a second wish, you always want to be more spectacular than the first wish was."

"Are you more spectacular?" Jeremy asked.

Steve walked over to the desk and knelt to be eye level with Jeremy. "Nope. I knew I couldn't be more spectacular, so I didn't even try."

Jeremy's eyes grew wide and he leaned toward Steve. "What did she wish for?"

Steve gently tapped him on the nose. "A little brother."

Jeremy leaned back and laughed. He turned to me as though I'd been silly. "Why wouldn't you tell me *that*?"

"I didn't want you to say anything to Mom and Dad. All this time they thought it was their idea."

"I won't tell them," he said.

Impulsively I bent down, picked Jeremy up, and hugged him. In the last month he'd grown so thin I could feel his ribs pressing through his shirt. "Everything has to go fine," I told him. "I can't lose my first wish."

He hugged me back, but only for a moment. Then he

slipped from my arms and climbed back onto the chair. Before anyone had a chance to say anything else, he squeezed his eyes shut. The words flew from his mouth. "This is my official third wish. I wish that no matter what happens with the cancer, my family will still be happy. Especially Annika." He opened his eyes. "Was it okay to add that last part? That's not cheating because it wasn't a different wish."

I couldn't answer him. It felt like I'd been hit with something. I just stared at Jeremy until I could get out, "That's not what you were supposed to wish for."

He shrugged. "I thought you needed the wish more. I don't want you to be sad anymore."

"But . . ." But everything I'd done meant nothing then. Only I couldn't say that, so the sentence hovered in the air, unfinished. Jeremy turned to Steve. "How come the genie didn't poof you away?"

"The genie thought I needed to stay and talk to Annika for a bit."

"Oh. Okay. I'm going to go tell Mom and Dad that you're not sad anymore. They were really worried about you before you came home."

He slid off the chair, gave Steve's legs one last hug, and then zoomed out of the room.

I watched him go, feeling the effects of my horrible defeat settling around me.

Steve put his hand on my arm. "This doesn't mean the surgery won't go well. It will probably go wonderfully."

I barely heard him. "Mom and Dad must have said things about me while I was gone, and they worried Jeremy. It's because I left to find you that he thought I needed the third wish more." The same trapped feeling of being in the underworld crept into my heart. "No matter what I do, I can't win."

"He loves you, Annika. That's a good thing, a real thing. The wishes were never real."

His sentence snapped me back into my room, back to the present. I nodded. I took deep breaths. "You're right. The surgery might still go well." I managed to smile. "Maybe one day when Jeremy and I are old, we'll laugh about all of this."

"And when you tell him the whole story, be sure not to leave out the part where Esme went flying into the fishpond."

I nodded.

Steve stayed for a while longer, giving me more words of encouragement. I kept nodding, but inside I felt hollow. I gave him his clothes and my cell phone number. He said he'd try to get some child-sized Merry Man clothes for Jeremy as soon as possible.

"Will you be okay tomorrow?" he asked me.

I nodded, but I wasn't sure.

He bent down and kissed me good-bye, and then I did feel like I was going to be okay. After all, I was clearly the luckiest girl alive. Things would go well tomorrow. They had to.

Chapter **17**

$\mathcal{I}$ didn't go to school on Friday. I wanted to go to the hospital with my family, and besides, my parents thought it would be best if I avoided school until people stopped talking about the pictures that had showed up on *Entertainment Tonight.* Because they did. Along with an interview with Karli Roller in which she blamed me for her breakup with Steve Raleigh. "I knew there was someone else on his mind. A woman can always tell."

Right. I doubted she could tell which way was up without using an elevator.

Madison had been the one to call and tell me that the interview was on TV, but a couple of my friends called my cell phone afterward. The conversations went like this:

Them: Hey, there's these pictures of Steve Raleigh with some mystery girl who looks a ton like you.

Me: Really?

Them: Yeah, besides the brown hair, she could be your twin.

Me (*making a note to myself that I need to bleach my hair back to blond before I see any of my friends*): Really?

Because I was not about to tell any of them the truth. I didn't want them flipping out or bugging me to meet him, and I certainly didn't want a repeat performance with the paparazzi. Of course, this didn't mean that I didn't want Steve to take me to prom, because, hey, how cool would that be?

My parents watched the interview with worried expressions. I think they half expected reporters to call our house. They didn't, much to Leah's disappointment. She was more than willing to go on TV and give an exclusive about Steve's trip to see us.

"People should know the truth about what a wonderful guy he is," she said.

"Jeremy shouldn't," I said, and that was the end of it. We all agreed that we wouldn't ever say anything about meeting a famous actor.

Mom conferred with one of her friends who was a hairdresser and who then came over and redid my hair. When she was done, it looked . . . blonder, but not like it had when I started out. My hair, apparently, was going to take time to recover.

Friday morning the entire family set off for Las Vegas to go to Sunrise Children's Hospital. Before school Madison had stopped by with a teddy bear for Jeremy and a hug for me. Her hair had already reverted to its natural color. It looked exactly the same. I envied the way she could glide back into her regular life.

On the trip to Las Vegas, I played cards with Jeremy, trying to squeeze out a few more moments of normal before we arrived at the hospital. "You never finished the story," he said to me. "What happened after the crows?"

Yes, what? He hadn't believed any of my supernatural attempts to escape. I decided to go with the obvious. "We decided to climb out. You know how sometimes we go to those rock-climbing walls? The cliff walls in the underworld are just like that. Well, except lots bigger."

"Then why doesn't everyone climb out?"

"Because the cliff walls are so steep and so tall most people give up after a while. But you wouldn't give up, would you?"

He looked at me, his eyes serious, and didn't answer.

"Promise me you won't ever give up, okay?"

His eyes stayed serious. "Doesn't the Grim Reaper catch people who try to climb out?"

"I'll distract him while you climb. You'll be fine."

I let him win the game. Then I let him win another. Perhaps it was the wrong thing to do. After he'd won the third game, he looked at me critically and whispered, "You're supposed to be happy—I wished it."

"Sometimes it takes a little while for a wish to kick in," I said.

"Like how Robin Hood didn't come right away?" he asked.

"Right. Like that."

"Okay. But you'll be happy soon . . . right?"

I hoped so, but I knew it could only be true if the surgery went well.

"I'll be happy if you don't give up," I said.

We reached the hospital and my parents signed Jeremy in. Then we waited. My parents went into a back room to go over insurance papers. Leah and I took turns reading him stories. Every once in a while, her voice caught in her throat, which made the situation feel even more painfully real. She was the one in the family who'd stayed the calmest about Jeremy's treatment, and now even she was breaking. I took her hand and squeezed it, just like I had when we were little girls.

My parents came out, and we waited again. The hospital had told us to be here at eleven-thirty—two hours before the surgery time. Apparently this was how long it took to do the paperwork. We all went back into a pre-op room, and the nurse took his blood pressure, weight, that sort of thing. Then Jeremy changed into hospital pajamas and got to play Nintendo while the nurse asked my parents questions. We waited some more. A child life specialist came in to explain the procedure to Jeremy. An anesthesiologist came in to talk to Jeremy and ask more questions.

I wondered how everyone could manage to sound so normal, so cheerful, when this was anything but.

Finally we walked out into the hallway, gave Jeremy a last hug, and they led him away.

"Keep climbing," I whispered, but he was too far away to hear me.

Twenty-eight people sat in the waiting room. I counted them, multiple times, in between staring into space and chewing my gum so hard that my jaw ached. I finally threw the gum out. Mom and Dad talked to each other in hushed voices. Leah flipped through pages of a magazine without reading any of it.

We waited, and waited, and waited.

I told my parents I needed to stretch my legs. I left the room and walked down the hallway slowly. Strangers went by me, washing past me like debris in a stream. I didn't know where to go. Eventually I ended up at the chapel. I peered at the door but didn't open it. When you're not on speaking terms with God, you don't drop by his house. He probably wouldn't be happy to see me.

People kept walking by me, but I didn't move.

Really, when one looked at all the horrible things in the world, what evidence did anyone have that God or a spiritual world existed?

But even as I thought of this possibility, I couldn't believe it. People weren't firecrackers who burst into the night sky with brilliance and glory, and a moment later faded away to nothing. Our souls had to be more lasting than that.

I thought—I nearly said the words out loud—"God, if you love me even a little bit, you'll make sure they get the whole tumor. You'll make it so my brother will be all right." Then I remembered I'd prayed like that right before Jeremy's first MRI.

And that hadn't turned out well; I obviously already knew the answer to whether God loved me. Still, I shut my eyes and whispered, "Please make him better." Then I walked back down the hall, listening to the squeak of my shoes against the floor.

I went back to the waiting room and watched the clock hands push forward. I heard every rustle of magazine pages being turned, like dry leaves crackling across pavement. Finally the doctor came into the room and asked to see my parents in one of the adjoining private rooms.

Leah and I weren't invited to that talk, but it didn't matter, I could tell the news as soon as I looked at the doctor's weary face.

Something had gone wrong.

I sat not moving, as though I could stop time this way, as though I could keep the bad news at bay if I turned to stone.

Twenty minutes went by. My father reappeared in the waiting room, his eyes rimmed with red. He motioned for Leah and me to follow him into the room. When we walked in, my mom wouldn't look at us. "They couldn't remove the entire tumor," Dad said. "It's too connected. It's already in vital parts of his brain. . . ."

He didn't say more, but we knew what he meant. The cancer would eventually win this battle. I couldn't bring myself to ask how long Jeremy had left. Was it months? Weeks?

I was wrong about not being able to cry. Because the tears came, instantly, relentlessly. I couldn't stop them. My dad hugged me, but it didn't help. I took a step backward, choking on emotion. I couldn't control any of it.

Finally I said, "I'm going out to the van," because I didn't like falling apart this way in front of my family.

I didn't walk, I ran through the hospital.

None of my efforts had made any difference. None of my prayers had been heard.

I will not go on, I thought. I won't. I will throw my soul to the wind and blow into a thousand pieces. I will wash up on a shore somewhere like bleached and broken driftwood. I will dry out in the sun until I—and any gift I ever had—shrivel into the sand.

I'm not sure how long I sat in the van. Long enough that my ribs ached from crying and the tears stopped coming. My thoughts didn't dry up as easily. I shut my eyes, trying to erase the phrase that pounded inside my mind: God, why don't you love me?

I heard the door open. I figured it was Dad, but when I looked up, it was Steve climbing inside.

"You came," I said. It was all I could get out.

He slid in beside me, his eyes full of consolation. "Ron booked a flight for me, remember?"

I did remember, but I figured Steve would change his plans since he came yesterday.

"I brought Jeremy his Merry Man things. The costume department whipped them together as soon as I told them why I needed them." He reached out and stroked my hair. "Your parents told me about the surgery. I'm so sorry."

I didn't answer. I just leaned toward him, and he hugged me. Neither of us spoke for a while.

When he pulled away from me, he said, "Your family is in the recovery room with Jeremy. You should be there with them when he wakes up."

"I can't." The words tore from my throat. "I know I'm supposed to be strong, and I'm supposed to go on somehow, but I don't want to. Ever. I want to be resentful and angry and destroy things." I didn't say the rest, which was that I wanted to hurt God. It sounded like an impossible task, as impossible as outwitting the Grim Reaper.

Steve ran his hand over my back. "Yesterday you asked me what the purpose of life is. I've thought about that ever since. I think it's to do good no matter what life throws at you, to not let the pain turn you bitter. It's something we have to learn, something we have to make ourselves become."

"What about little kids who die? What's their purpose, then?"

"Little kids don't have to learn it. They already know." Steve laid his hand over mine. "You're not going to turn bitter, because Jeremy wants you to be happy. That's what he used his last wish for. You've got to at least try."

I didn't answer or even look at him. I knew he was right, but I couldn't put on happiness like it was a sweater or something.

"Think of one thing to be happy for. Just one thing." As he said this, I realized he spoke from experience. He'd pushed through devastation at some point, and now was passing on survival advice.

"But nothing makes up for this," I said.

"I know, but you can find something to be glad about every day. He loves you, that's a big thing."

And then I knew his devastation had been his fight with his family. It was easier to talk about them than it was to talk about Jeremy. My voice became steadier. "Your parents do love you. Before I left, your mom gave me a hug and told me to take good care of you."

His eyebrows rose. "She hugged you? She didn't even hug me."

"She might have if you hadn't stormed off."

He tilted his head, surveying me. "What did you say to them anyway? When I got back home, they'd left a message on my answering machine. My mom said she hoped I had a good trip, and my father came very close to apologizing for being short-tempered during my visit. It's not like them at all."

"I didn't tell them anything that wasn't real, or at least true."

"Uh-huh." I knew he didn't believe me, but he smiled anyway.

I gave his hand a squeeze. "I'm happy you came."

Steve glanced down at his watch. "And I'd better get changed. Robin Hood has to deliver the clothes."

"Tell my parents I'll come in when my eyes unswell. I don't want Jeremy to see me this way."

He nodded. "I'll tell them."

I watched him stride across the parking lot and into the hospital. I tried to think of all the things I had to be happy about. A family who loved me. More time with

Jeremy, even if it was a short time. I couldn't think of anything after that because I started crying again.

I would never make it into the hospital at this rate.

Half an hour later, Steve came out dressed in his Robin Hood costume, drawing the attention of every person in the parking lot.

He opened the van door and held his hand out to me. "Jeremy is awake and asking for you."

"I can't go like this," I said, but I got out of the van. "I won't even be able to talk coherently."

"That doesn't matter to him," Steve said.

When we walked inside the hospital room, all I could think about was how little Jeremy looked in the hospital bed. White gauze wrapped around his head, covering the wound.

He saw me and lifted his head a fraction. This must have hurt because he immediately rested his head again. He waved me over. The medication slurred his voice, but I could still sense his excitement. "Annika, you don't have to worry about your story anymore. I know how it ends."

My heart stopped. I couldn't speak. What had they told him about his condition?

"I dreamt about it," he said. "I went to the underworld, and I climbed up the walls like you told me."

His words painted an immediate picture in my mind.

I could see the dark cliffs and Jeremy's tiny figure pressed against them, climbing. Ragged peaks towered above him, harsh, imposing, presenting an impossible task.

"I didn't see you, I didn't see anyone. I was all alone, but I knew the Grim Reaper was waiting at the bottom, and I didn't want to stay with him."

I saw Jeremy's fingers grasping to find handholds on the cold rock wall, but he was slipping. He wouldn't be able to hold on. I knew this, and I couldn't help him.

"I'm so sorry," I said.

"I thought I would fall," he said, "but then a big light came, and God took hold of my hand. He said I didn't have to climb anymore because I could fly." Jeremy sounded quite proud he knew something I didn't. "So you don't have to worry about how to get out of the underworld. God takes care of that."

I saw this too, saw Jeremy surrounded by light and for a moment felt that God turned and looked at me—not with reproach, but with a smile of love.

Then I was back in the hospital room, breathless and blinking.

"That's a beautiful story," I said, as much to myself as to Jeremy. "That's exactly the right ending."

From beside me Steve took hold of my hand and squeezed it. I held on to his hand but kept my eyes on Jeremy. "I'll tell you as many stories as you want when we get home."

"Tell me some of me as a Merry Man," he said.

"Oh, you're the best Merry Man. You have lots of adventures. Robin Hood takes you everywhere, and you shoot better than everyone."

"Good." He let out a happy sigh, and glanced at Steve and me with a sly smile. "Don't worry," he whispered. "I won't tell Maid Marion about you."

"Thanks," I said. Then I bent over and gave Jeremy a kiss.

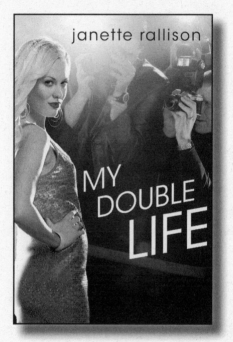